S0-BEB-428

With Hitler in New York

With Hitler in New York

And Other Stories

by Richard Grayson

TAPLINGER PUBLISHING COMPANY • New York

Grateful acknowledgement is made to the following magazines and anthologies in which these stories first appeared: *Shenandoah, Confrontation, Carleton Miscellany, Epoch, Writ, Junction, Zone, riverrun, Student Lawyer, Dark Horse, Boxspring, Statements 2: New Fiction, Tailings, Phantasm, Contrast, Calvert, Uroboros, Bellingham Review, Dragon Fire, Ataraxia, The Small Pond, Mikrokosmos, Star-Web Paper, Willmore City, Chouteau Review, Paris Voices.*

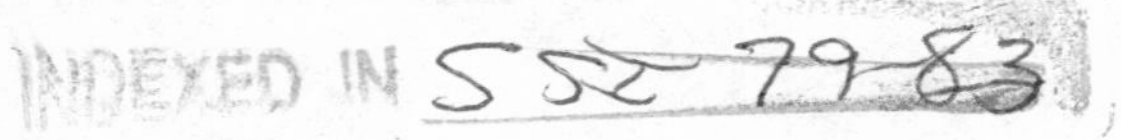

First edition

Library of Congress Catalog No. 78-20695

ISBN 0-8008-8406-X

9 8 7 6 5 4 3 2 1

Contents

Introduction

With Hitler In New York 13
Ordinary Man 23
Chief Justice Burger, Teen Idol 27
Lincoln On the Couch 33
Real People 39

Objects

In the Lehman Collection 45
Infant Sorrow 50
Peninsular People 54
Triptych 59
Classified Personal 63

Families

Wednesday Night at Our House 69
Slowly, Slowly in the Wind 81
On the Boardwalk 86
Notes Toward a Story For Uncle Irving 92
Driving Slow 98

Women

The Princess From the Land of Porcelain 103
Aspects of Ann 111
Kirchbachstrasse 121, 2800 Bremen 115

Subjects

The Art of Living 123
Garibaldi in Exile 128
Au Milieu Interieur 135
The Mother in My Bedroom 144

Artifacts

The Finest Joe Colletti Story Ever Written (So Far) 149
"But In a Thousand Other Worlds" 155
What *Really* Happened in Cambodia 162
"Go Not to Lethe" Celebrates its 27th Anniversary 169
The First Annual James V. Forrestal Memorial Lecture 180

To my parents
and Wesley Strick

Introduction

When my uncle Red Sarachek was dying of lung cancer I had to force myself to look at him and not think of the expression *a shadow of his former self.* He called me over sometimes because he knew I knew where to get the marijuana that his doctors said would ease the pain of the chemotherapy treatments. Uncle Red would sit in his paneled den and I would roll a joint for us. The stereo would be playing the Boston Pops. It would be snowing outside. I would be teaching Uncle Red how to drag on the joint.

"A hell of a thing," he would say. "It was smoking that got me into this mess." And he'd shudder and inhale the marijuana and hold it in what was left of his lungs. Then we'd get silly and say strange things and confide in each other as uncles and nephews rarely do and we'd laugh and sometimes we'd start crying over nothing at all.

After Uncle Red died I found it hard to smoke marijuana anymore. When it was offered to me at parties I'd just shake my head no. Occasionally I would take a puff of someone else's joint, but I never bought it for myself again. It had served its purpose for me.

I have bad skin. I don't quite know how I got bad skin, but I have it, and I suppose I don't make the best of it. Even on days when my face is fairly clear I search the mirror for imperfections and I squeeze and pull at them until they are red and somewhat bigger than they were before. Sometimes when I squeeze the skin very hard a small bruise develops and in the morning I have a purple mark. Other times the scab turns a sickly shade of green with a black spot in the middle. I have tried everything that has come out on the market, over or under the counter: Listerex, Vanoxide, Stridex, Clearasil, Kiehl's Golden Seal Face Cream. Nothing seems to work. When I had a girlfriend she was into herbs and used to mix me a tea made out of lemon grass and lavender. She would give it to me warm and I'd drink half of it and spread the other half on a washcloth and lie down for an hour with the washcloth over my face. I was in heaven from the smell of lemon grass and lavender, but it did my skin no good. My girlfriend also made me a camomile rinse for my hair, which she said was good for blondes, and it was. It left my hair smelling like green apples and she would play with it for hours afterward. I have never liked public displays of affection in others, but when she used to play with my hair and there were people around, I never minded it one bit.

When I was in the second grade the teacher wanted me to get out of my shell and join the Cub Scouts, but I didn't want to. One day the teacher came over to me with a note she said I was to give to my mother. I thought it was about getting out of my shell again, but it was only a note saying that the teacher thought I needed glasses for the blackboard. My mother took me to an eye doctor, an old German lady who yelled at me for reading too much. She would berate me every year when I went into her office and she had to give me a new and stronger prescription. When I started going to Hebrew school, she was particularly upset because the letters in Hebrew prayer books were so small. The eye doctor would put eye drops in my eyes and warn me not to read anything for at least twenty-four hours. I would always find this intolerable and so I'd have to cajole my mother and my Uncle Red and my Aunt Tillybird to read articles in the encyclopedia to me. Once I went out and bought myself a comic book and read it when I wasn't supposed to, because of the eye drops. But I couldn't help it. It was my favorite comic book, The Justice League of America, and it had a cover with all the Justice League superheroes trapped inside a diamond and Green Arrow taking aim with a diamond-tipped arrow to rescue them. After he rescued them, they all asked him to join the Justice League of America and he said okay. I always wondered why he wasn't insulted that they hadn't ever asked him to join earlier.

My girlfriend and I would always wind up in the basement on a Friday night. She was a virgin and she didn't want to let me make love to her and we almost broke up over that many times. I had had several sexual experiences before that, but they were with girls I didn't particularly care for. Even if she didn't sleep with me, I was crazy about my girlfriend. And she let me get on top of her with just our jeans on and we'd go up and down and kiss and touch and it always seemed to me better than with any of the girls I'd actually laid. She almost always had an orgasm, and that had not happened with any of the others even though with them it was real sex. We'd perspire like crazy and strange farting noises would be caused by the movement of my chest and her breasts. She and I would laugh at the sounds. She was the only girl I ever met who could crack up in the middle of sex—or what was almost sex—and it would make you love her even more. We stayed out so late on Fridays, dry-humping in the basement and listening to Cat Stevens and talking about the stupidest things that somehow fascinated only the two of us in all the world; we stayed out so late that we both were never good for very much all day Saturday. I'd drive her home at five or six in the morning and we'd be shivering in my car and I'd hug her sometimes for twenty minutes before I'd let her go up to her house. When I got home again I'd eat a bagel plain, without even slicing it, and I'd have some pineapple juice, my favorite drink. Then I'd get into bed and masturbate even though my cock was so sore and it was always very good, thinking about her in her bed in her house.

After Uncle Red died I went into some sort of daze, I guess, and then I started getting all these crazy fears about going out places. Now I know it was agoraphobia, a kind of generalized fear of everything in the outside world. But then I only knew I was afraid of fainting or doing something embarrassing on the subway or in class or at the movies, so I pretty much stopped doing all those things for awhile. I was ashamed of myself for not being able to face the outside world, and I couldn't let anyone know that I was being such a baby. Luckily I caught mononucleosis, and although it was a very mild case, I let it drag on for months without stirring from my room. My mother and my Aunt Tillybird used to knock and come in and sit on the corner of my bed and tell me that I was the man of the family and men face things like their fears. I had to tell my girlfriend I didn't want to see her any more and that was a lie. Partially I didn't want to burden her with my problems, especially because she was having a rough time with her parents getting a divorce, but mostly I was just ashamed and didn't feel worthy to be her boyfriend. She used to write me letters and call me and finally I had to have Aunt Tillybird change the number to an unlisted one. I never answered her letters. I just lay in my bed trying to sleep. When I slept I had nightmares.

With Hitler In New York

HITLER'S GIRLFRIEND AND I are waiting for him in the International Arrivals Building at Kennedy Airport. Ellen and I stand in front of the West Customs Area. My brother is standing in front of the East Customs Area. He is waiting for my parents. My parents and Hitler have each landed at the same time, at seven o'clock. My parents are flying KLM from Saint Martin. Hitler is flying Laker from London and Manchester. He couldn't afford any other airline. He had to book his flight forty-five days in advance. But Laker paid for the ferry to England and the train ride to London as well. It is, as Hitler has written me, "a pretty good deal."

Next to us there is an old Englishwoman. She is clucking her tongue. We are watching the passengers of an Alitalia flight from Rome come out of Customs and hug and kiss and cry and carry on.

"These people are just disgraceful," the old Englishwoman says. "You'll see that the people from Laker will be much better behaved."

Ellen and I look at each other and decide to move away.

Ellen gets worried because Hitler has not yet come out. She is playing with her long blonde strands of hair. When she puts a bit of hair in her mouth, I tell her to stop it. Then she sees Hitler coming out of Customs.

He looks handsomer than I remembered him as being. He is smiling. When he gets to us, he hugs Ellen. He is so much taller than she.

I ask Hitler if I can carry his backpack.

"No, no, it's all right," he says in English.

Ellen tells Hitler in German that it's very hot outside and that he should take off his leather jacket. Hitler replies in English that he prefers to keep the jacket on.

When we go outside Hitler says of the heat, "It's like a bathroom."

On the ride back to Brooklyn, Hitler talks only English. It seems to be coming back to him now. Driving up Flatbush Avenue, we pass a bank that advertises its "Tellerphone" service, and Hitler asks what that is. I tell him it's a checking account where you can pay your bills by phone.

"But don't you have to say a code so they know it's you?" says Ellen from the back seat.

"Sure," I say. "Either a word or a series of numbers or letters."

Hitler smiles. "A commercial mantra, eh?"

I am surprised Hitler is so quick. Obviously I have been underestimating him all these years.

Hitler has to stay with the Judsons because Ellen's parents won't permit him to stay with them. The Judsons are wonderful people. Libby teaches swimming at the YWCA; she is Ellen's best friend in America, apart from myself. Mrs. Judson is a delightful woman, daughter of Ukrainian immigrants, a happily deserted wife. The Judsons live in a brownstone in Park Slope.

When we get to the Judsons' house, Hitler finally takes off his leather jacket. It is about ninety degrees. He takes off his work shirt too. Underneath he has a T-shirt that has shrunk just a little bit. Hitler is very skinny but he is tall. When I ask him what the air smells like up there, he says "Dwarfs," and we all laugh.

We watch TV for a little while in the Judsons' living room. It is a pilot for a projected series starring Barbara Feldon. Hitler only likes the commercials. When he sees Senator Sam Ervin doing a commercial for American Express, Hitler really freaks out.

"Imagine Willy Brandt doing a commercial for Beck's Beer," he says to Ellen. She explains that German television is very different. All the commercials are on at one time, for only forty minutes a day.

Libby says we should all sit outside and eat ice cream. Ellen has dope that she bought from my brother and we all sit out on the stoop smoking a joint and eating vanilla ice cream. Hitler regales us with stories about his Sunday stopover in London. Ellen tells us that Hitler thinks the English people are so stiff and formal.

"It was tea everywhere," Hitler says. He has a nice air about him, as though he is so comfortable with his body. I think I would like to be like him. "We went to this pub, and then they took me to see this movie, 'Black Emanuelle.' It was so silly, no? There were strange scenes in the bathroom and finally I got up and said to Clive and Zbyczek, 'You don't really want to stay, do you?' They said no, but really they did."

We go back into the living room, the only air-conditioned room in the Judsons' house. Mrs. Judson is watching "Eyewitness News." They are still talking about the blackout and the looting.

Hitler says he is sorry he missed the blackout. "It would have been, sort of, an adventure," he tells us, and then we say how awful it was.

"This heat wave is bad enough," Libby tells Hitler, but he has started to doze off on the couch.

"Poor thing," Mrs. Judson says. We bring down the foldaway bed and wake Hitler up so he can get in it.

"What do you think of Hitler?" Ellen asks me as I take her to her parents' house. We are driving along the Belt Parkway at midnight with our car windows wide open, but there is not a hint of a breeze.

"I kind of like him," I say. "I never realized he was so witty."

Ellen kisses me on the cheek at her parents' house. I watch to see that she gets in safely.

The next day it reaches 100 degrees, a record-breaker. Hitler is uncomfortable. He hasn't slept much and he has jet lag. In addition, he seems to be getting a cold.

He and Ellen have gotten breakfast at McDonald's. Hitler likes fast food and there are no fast food places in Germany. When I get over to the Judsons', Ellen and Hitler are watching a movie on Channel 9. Hitler is lying under the covers.

"I think I'm going to go to the Apex Technical School," Hitler says. He has obviously seen the commercials for it. "To repair air conditioners in this climate must be profitable." I chuckle.

The news comes on and all the talk is about the heat wave. A woman reporter asks an official if we will have a "water blackout." Hitler gets out of bed, puts on his jeans, and we go pick up Libby at the YWCA.

Libby, Ellen, Hitler and I have dinner at Shakespeare's in the Village. It is air conditioned. Hitler has a salad because he is not in the mood for meat. Libby has onion soup and bread because she is a vegetarian. Ellen and I have hamburgers.

When the lights flicker for a moment, Hitler gets excited. He so hopes for another blackout.

After dinner, around nine, we walk to Washington Square. It is almost cool. We sit at the edge of the fountain, facing outwards. Hitler and Ellen are holding hands; so are Libby and I.

A black man with no shirt on comes over to us and says we look stoned. We smile and he asks us if we need more dope to get stoned on.

"We are stoned on the evening," Hitler tells the black man. He goes away shaking his head.

When I get home, I see my father in his bedroom. He looks very small. I come in to apologize to him for not seeing him since he got back from vacation. I have been spending most of my time with Hitler.

"Grandpa's very sick," my father tells me. "He had another heart attack. He's in a coma."

"Oh, no," I say. I think about the phone call I got from my grandfather on Sunday, and how he begged me to visit him in Florida.

I pick up Hitler and Ellen at the Kings Highway station and take them back to my house, to my swimming pool. I am still worried about my grandfather.

Hitler and Ellen enjoy the water. He is so much bigger than she is that he throws her under constantly. She cries for help, and I know she doesn't like it, but I pretend she is just joking. I do not want to spoil Hitler's fun.

"You're a sadist, you know that?" Ellen says to Hitler after they get out of the pool. Hitler shrugs. Then Ellen turns to me. "He did the same thing to me in Greece last year," she says.

Hitler and I are going to Ellen's parents' house for dinner. I let Hitler take a shower and use my razor and shaving cream so he can impress Ellen's mother, who has never liked him. My own mother seems to like Hitler. She is pleased that he doesn't mess up the bathroom.

The three of us arrive at Ellen's parents', and Hitler and I have to wait outside because Ellen's grandfather, visiting from Florida, has to put on a pair of pants.

Dinner is dairy: bagels, tuna salad, corn on the cob, lettuce and tomatoes and iced tea. It is too hot to eat a heavy meal. Ellen's mother doesn't talk to Hitler except to say, "Pass me that salt bagel." Ellen's father tries to joke around. Her grandfather tells us about his meeting with an old black woman customer of his from years ago, when he sold appliances on credit.

The old black woman's name was Mother Brown. Ellen's grandfather walked up four flights to see her, and when he opened the door, Mother Brown got so excited that she ran over and hugged him. Then she started crying. "Mr. Glass, I'm so *old*!" she said. And Ellen's grandfather said, "Why, you're only eighty, I'm three years older than you."

Across the table Hitler winks at me.

After dinner we go to visit Mike. Mike has just had corrective surgery for a separated shoulder. He comes down wearing no shirt, and the scar looks ugly. They only took the bandage off the day before.

Hitler and I have to shake Mike's left hand.

Mike's mother comes out and kisses Ellen. Later Ellen will say that Mike's mother always wanted him to marry Ellen because they were both Jewish.

Mike's mother practically ignores Hitler, so we decide to take a walk to the beach.

Above the Belt Parkway we smoke a joint. I cough, as usual.

"Look at all the cars," Hitler says. "Each one of them has someone going somewhere."

"I'm really stoned," Mike says.

"I'm thirsty," Ellen says.

"Let's go have eggcreams," I say.

And we do.

After our eggcreams, we go on the boardwalk. Ellen tells Hitler that there are many old people and Soviet Jews in Brighton Beach and cautions him not to talk German. Hitler nods.

We join a circle surrounding a fiftyish woman in shorts. She is very animatedly singing a Yiddish folk song. All of the old people are enjoying it. It seems like it's supposed to be funny, or maybe dirty. Hitler is listening intently.

"*Farshteit?*" I ask Hitler.

"*Ja, ja,*" he says. "She is telling about how not to have children."

An old lady next to us smiles. She seems glad that Hitler understands the song. We walk away before she can recognize him.

Libby and Mike are sitting on a boardwalk bench, talking about old times.

Hitler and I are leaning against the rail, watching the dark ocean, the dark sand, talking about this and that.

"Giscard d'Estaing is so funny," Hitler says. "The things he does to make himself popular."

I nod.

I tell Hitler I can name all ten states of West Germany. He counts on his fingers as I name them. I can only name nine. I know the other one has a hyphenated name, but it is difficult.

"It's where Stuttgart is," Hitler gives me a hint.

Now I remember. "Baden-Württemburg," I tell him, and Hitler smiles.

I wonder if I am beginning to fall in love with him.

On Friday night Hitler gives me a present, a book of Rilke's poems. He tells me not to worry about my grandfather, who is still in a coma.

We eat dinner at a Szechuan restaurant in Brooklyn Heights, Hitler, Ellen, Libby and me. We order four dishes and take from each other's plates. We eat with chopsticks. Hitler likes Cantonese spareribs, but we will have to get them another time. The oranges and fortune cookies make a fine dessert. We are very full.

When the check comes, we just divide it by four. No one seems to object. Libby, Ellen, and I give Hitler our share and he pays for the meal with a fifty-dollar traveler's check. He forgets to leave a tip and they call him back for that.

The four of us walk off our dinner by the Brooklyn Heights Promenade. We look at that night view of the lower Manhattan skyline.

"The most gorgeous cliché in America," I say.

It is actually chilly. The heat wave has broken.

Hitler is hugging Ellen and Libby. They come over to me and they hug me too. We are standing by the rail, all touching each other. It is a very fine moment.

We have walked off our dinner by looking at the brownstones on Hicks Street. We are ready for dessert. The four of us drive to Atlantic Avenue, to the Seeds of the Future Café, a health-food place run by young black women.

Hitler orders Asantiwa's Carrot Cake and peppermint tea. They do not have Beck's Beer, which is what he really wanted.

Someone at another table, a Filipino, recognizes Hitler. But everything is too mellow for him to make a scene.

My grandfather dies.

My father goes down to Florida to bring back the body for

the funeral. My grandmother is coming back too.

It is Saturday night, the big party Libby is giving for Hitler. I cannot miss it.

I don't tell anyone that my grandfather has died.

I get stoned with Hitler and Ellen.

The guests arrive.

Everyone seems to be getting along.

Hitler is making a big hit with everyone.

If I were capable of being jealous of him, I would be. But by now I love him too much.

Hitler drinks bottle after bottle of Beck's Beer. He once worked at the brewery in Bremen. "Just think," he says. "Maybe I once saw this bottle pass me by on the assembly line in Germany."

I try my best to smile.

A fortyish ad agency executive, someone's lover, comes by and says, "Look how that Nazi can drink so much beer and still stay thin." He pinches the flab on my stomach. "Fatties like us," he says, speaking of me and him, "just look at beer and gain weight."

When he goes away, I tell Hitler that he has hurt my feelings.

"He did not do it voluntarily, I am sure," Hitler says.

Ellen comes over and takes photographs of me and Hitler, our arms around each other.

Hitler gives Ellen many kisses.

We get drunk and I tell Hitler that we should plan to win the Nobel Prize the same year, he for Peace, I for Literature.

"We would have to wear ties," he says.

"No, tuxedos," I tell him. "And top hats and canes."

"And we could get up on the platform and sing, 'There's No Business like Show Business . . .' The Swedish Academy would be talking about us for a long while, eh?" Hitler's nose is very red.

Libby gets sick and the party begins to end.

I drive Ellen back to her parents', and Hitler comes along for the ride. I look away as they say goodnight. They are going back to Germany in two days.

Driving Hitler back to the Judsons' house, I remember my grandfather's death.

On Ocean Parkway I begin to cry.

"Do not have tears," Hitler says. He asks what is wrong.

We pull over to a side street and I tell him.

He says he is sorry.

Then he tells me things to try to make me laugh. How a tattooed sailor in New Orleans once offered to support him for a year. How Libby's mother used hair spray instead of antiperspirant after her shower that morning. How Ellen looks when she wakes up after an all-night drunk.

I feel a little better and begin driving back to Park Slope.

At the Judsons' door I ask Hitler if he ever feels bitter.

"Useless," he says.

I do not know if he is talking about anger or himself or myself. In the end it doesn't matter.

Hitler puts his hand on my shoulder and tells me to sleep well.

Ordinary Man

WHEN I WAS A YOUNG BOY the planet Xenon exploded. My father, the scientist Moh-el, sent me in a rocketship to Earth. I was found by a kindly old couple, the Weinglasses, and raised as their own son. At about puberty something funny began to happen. The Weinglasses realized it too and when I was eighteen they sent me off to a place called the State University of New York at Stony Brook. It was there that I discovered my powers.

I was taking an anthropology exam one day when suddenly I began to cry uncontrollably. "What's wrong with you?" the proctor demanded. "I don't know," I wailed. She sent me off to the counseling department to see the shrink, old irascible Doc White. Doc White figured it out right away.

"You were born on Xenon with its twin blue suns," the old man told me as I lay on his couch sobbing. "Therefore you have special emotional powers. You feel things more deeply than anyone else. You are like a super-manic-depressive."

"Oh shit," I cried.

"You should use these powers for the good of society," said Doc White. "With me guiding you, you can become a great force in fighting evildoers. I'll design a costume for you and whenever something is wrong, I'll call on you with my secret watch that buzzes at 50-minute intervals. You can become . . . Ordinary Man!"

I was hesitant at first. All I really wanted was to become a market analyst. But the idea of a secret identity intrigued me. I never liked the name the Weinglasses had given me—Stanley—and here was a chance to be someone else. Wonderful. The uniform fit me like a glove, except for the gloves, which were a little too tight for my oversized Xenon hands. But I was proud to be Ordinary Man. My baptism of fire soon occurred.

Doc White was being brought up on charges before the faculty review board. He was accused of making advances to several female students who had been referred to him for counseling. These charges were trumped up by Doc White's arch-enemy, Chairman Should of the Psychology Department. I entered the hearing room through a window, surprised the sitting review board, and proceeded to have a nervous breakdown—a nervous breakdown the likes of which those professors had never seen. I cried, I ranted, I threw papers around, I pulled out my own hair, I banged my head on their table, I screamed bloody death, I made grotesque faces, I swore, I pleaded, I cajoled, I insisted, I attacked various board members with my hands and every available textbook. Ordinary Man was acquitting himself well.

And Doc White was acquitted too. The review board dismissed all charges against him, and the coeds who had made false accusations were suspended. Doc White was jubilant. "Thank you, Ordinary Man!" he cried out, winking one of his rheumy eyes at me.

But Chairman Should shook his fist at me in fury. "You'll pay for this, young man!" he shouted. "I'll get my revenge!"

And he did. Doc White was found dead of a stroke two months later. As Stanley Weinglass, I was powerless to do anything. But as Ordinary Man—well, I worked myself into the worst depression ever recorded in the annals of Long Island psychiatry. I lay inert for three weeks, crying and saying, "What's the use of going on?" My foster parents were called for, but they couldn't control the situation at all. "Pretend like everything's all right, darling," said my foster mother. "You got to get so excited over some old teacher dropping dead?" said my foster father. I just lay there, saying nothing. Finally they went back home to the Bronx.

I lay in my bed for another six weeks. I was as inert as xenon, the inert gas which gave my native planet its name. Then, during one of my lengthy naps, I dreamed of Doc White.

He appeared before my very eyes. "Great Sigmund's ghost!" the shrink railed. "Are you going to stay in this depression forever? Even Ordinary Man has to snap out of it sometime! Revenge me against my enemy, Chairman Should! Do it for old Doc White, boy!"

That did it. There and then, I flew off my bed and went to the home of Chairman Should. Little did I reckon with the fact that he had been prepared for my arrival all the time I had been depressed.

Chairman Should had an ape waiting for me in his foyer. Not an ordinary ape, but Mendal Gorilla from the golf-playing gorillas. He was enormous and hairy and he had a terrific backswing which he used on me at the first opportunity he had. I was knocked cold.

When I came to, I was in Chairman Should's experimental psychology lab—the scene of hundreds of inquisitions against white mice and guinea pigs. I was strapped to a couch while the fiendish Chairman Should knelt beside me with a giant syringe in his hands.

"This is lithium," he cackled. "Enough lithium to stabilize even San Francisco!"

I scrunched up my face in horror.

"Scared, huh?" said my torturer.

In response I spit phlegm all over the Chairman, blinding him temporarily. "You didn't reckon with my sinus condition!" I shouted as I burst free of my bonds.

In a manic state, I watched my cute face in the mirror.

"You've done it again, Ordinary Man!" I told myself. "Now you can go on talk shows and become famous. You can play Vegas for big money. You can get government grants, anything! The world is your oyster!"

"Not so fast," my reflection said back to me. "Ordinary Man must not be put to use for commercial purposes. No, he can make more people feel guilty if they see how hard he fights evil and how much he suffers, getting nothing in return for all his troubles."

"You're right!"

"I'm always right!"

And I ended the discussion with myself on a high note, wondering if I had discovered yet another secret power: schizophrenia.

So now I keep watch over all Long Island. Chairman Should may be gone, but there are always those who want to victimize and manipulate and fuck the minds of those less stable than they. Ordinary Man fights for the rights of all neurotics and psychotics. With me around, they don't have to worry any more than they ought to—which is a hell of a lot anyway.

Chief Justice Burger, Teen Idol

WARREN'S GOT A KEY PROBLEM!

Warren has a problem?! Oh, don't worry, it's nothing serious . . . . . most of the time, anyway! Warren's just a little forgetful–when it comes to his keys!

IF THE CHIEF JUSTICE was your dinner date, you'd be very wise in watching every move he made right after paying the check and getting ready to take you home. Why? Because more than once, in fact, *very* often, Warren Burger's been known to leave his keys sitting on the table of a restaurant or he's forgotten where he put them!

He's not sure what it means, but he's positive he's got something inside of him that refuses to have any recollection when it comes to a set of keys! It doesn't matter where he is, either . . . because it hasn't just happened to him on dates!

Warren's left his keys locked inside his desk at the Supreme Court Building, on an airplane heading for the ABA convention, in Eric Sevareid's house—you name it and the Chief Justice has probably forgotten his keys there! Now, Warren's always promising himself that he's going to have extra sets made up so he can pass them out to fellow Justices Potter Stewart and "Whizzer" White. He figures that if his keys are misplaced *then,* he can always call up one of them and his problems are over!

He hasn't exactly gotten around to *doing* it yet, though, so adorable Warren is still in a jam. One Thursday after studying briefs on a Milwaukee school-integration case, the Chief Justice was going to drive home, throw some things into an overnight bag and rush out to catch a plane to Key Biscayne where Bebe Rebozo (former President Nixon's pal) was waiting to take Warren sailing on his yacht for the weekend.

There was just one catch, and that was that Warren had to be at the dock in Florida by a certain time, otherwise they couldn't leave until the next morning! Warren rushed home, jumped out of his limousine and ran to the front door. But he didn't have his house key with him and nobody else was home! Where was his house key? Warren didn't know and by *then* (time was running out!), he didn't have a spare moment to find out!

He caught a jet at Dulles Airport and arrived in Key Biscayne just in time to spend the entire weekend without a change of clothing. The poor Chief Justice, his forgetfulness really cost him *that* day! Bebe Rebozo had a good laugh about it, and Warren, too, went along with it like the good sport he is.

But good sport or no good sport, Warren's got to get down to business and work out a solution to his "keyed-up" problem. In the meantime, he's dispensing his special brand of justice the way only *he* can. Just be grateful that the one key Chief Justice Burger *can't* lose is the key to your heart!

LETTERS TO THE EDITOR

SO SORRY

I know it's a little late, but it's because I didn't know how to say it. I'm a Warren Burger fan, and I love him very much. I have to admit I was jealous when I heard how much time he was spending with Agatha Christie, but now I want to tell Warren "I'm sorry" about the fact that she died. She must've been really nice and Warren must have liked her very much. All my friends and I want to send our sympathies to you, Warren.

F.L., T.P., L.D., AND Y.F.
Buffalo, N.Y.

EQUAL TIME

To the girl who said that Warren WASN'T a fantastic judge and legal scholar, I just want to say two words. The first is "You're" and the second is "NUTS"! If you haven't read his opinions maybe I'll apologize, but if you have, then "nuts" is the only word for you! My friends agree.

ROBIN OF DENVER

WARREN READ MY NAME

One Monday I heard the Supreme Court decisions, like always they were great. But in this one opinion Warren read the case: *Nebraska v. Terry* (Terry's my name!). I know there's other girls with the same name and the decision was about property taxes, but it made me feel terrific to know he kept reading my name. I was just sitting there, then he said "Terry" and my heart almost popped out. When it comes to Warren's legal opinion my heart always skips a beat.

TERRY SMITH
Salt Lake City

WONDERFUL WARREN

Ever since Warren Burger was a Federal Appeals Judge, I've been in love with him. I was so crushed when he was in the minority in the Pentagon Papers case that I couldn't eat for three days. I always try to keep tabs on Warren, but sometimes I slip up and miss a speech he gives somewhere. He's so busy that it's hard to keep up with him.

BETH B. OF MIAMI

BELIEVE IT OR NOT

Attention Connie S., who had a letter in your September issue. I personally weighed John Marshall, Oliver Wendell Holmes, Louis Brandeis and Hugo Black on one side of the scale of justice, and Warren Burger on the other side and guess who came out *numero uno?* Why, Warren, of course! He's loaded with everything and will always come out on top.

Learned H.

LOVES BURGER RULINGS

Please have more and more and more about wonderful Warren Burger and his decisions on right-to-work laws! I could listen to him talk about collective bargaining until my ears fall off. I read all his rulings till my eyes pop out. More on Warren—my heart's already popped out for him.

Sally Westerfield

FIRST TIME OFFERED!

"The Secret of Warren Burger"
AN UNAUTHORIZED BIOGRAPHY
A Complete Book Loaded With Photos and Facts

Now you can know all about the guy who lights up the legal scene! Find out the true story of how Warren grew up in Minneapolis, the son of average middle-class parents. Learn how Warren worked his way through St. Paul College of Law and how he struggled to pass the bar exams. Share moments of happiness and tears as Warren works his way up from the municipal bench to the highest judicial office in the land. THE TRUE FACTS ARE ALL HERE!

You'll find answers to all of these questions:
—What does he do with his private moments?
—How does he feel about reapportionment?
—Is he a strict constructionist?
—What is Warren really like?
—Does he have a steady girl?
—Can you meet him in person?

DON'T WAIT!! BE THE FIRST TO READ THIS ONE-OF-A-KIND BOOK. NOT ON SALE IN STORES! AVAILABLE THROUGH THE MAIL ONLY!

WARREN TELLS ALL!

Dear Warren,

I loved your speech on judicial reform to the NAACP Convention. All my friends thought it was really neat. I can't wait to see a book-length compilation of all your grooviest speeches—can you tell me when it will be out and what speeches you'll be putting in it? Thanks!

BRENDA

Dear Brenda,

Hey, thank you! I'm glad you and your friends liked my judicial reform speech so much—it was really fun to deliver. My collection of speeches should be out around Christmastime and I'm very excited about it! Some of the speeches will be on due process, others on the effects of recent court rulings on labor contracts, but I don't want to tell *too* much about it, I want it to be a surprise.

Dear Warren,

What would you do if the Supreme Court voted 8–1 on a case and you were the only justice dissenting? I can't imagine that *ever* happening, but I'm curious to know.

RANDI

Dear Randi,

I'd probably sit down and cry. Only kidding! I'd probably feel hurt for a while and then try to forget it.

Dear Warren,

I know how super you and your mom get along and I think that's great! But do you ever get into arguments with her, like if she thinks you're wrong on capital punishment or things like that. I'm just curious, I hope it's not too personal.

Best,
SUSI

Dear Susi,

You're right, my mom and I do get along great and I know she's always there when I need her. She's very supportive of me and the whole family. But we're just like anybody else and there *are* times—like in a recent decision on pensions—when we disagree. I usually take her opinions into consideration but figure I know what's best for the country. That's usually the end of the argument! Thanks for writing, Susi, and I hope you keep following what's happening on the Court! Keep smiling!

COMING NEXT MONTH . . .

EVERYTHING YOU EVER WANTED TO KNOW ABOUT WARREN BURGER!

—Secret facts
—Complete judicial record
—How to make him love you

Lincoln on the Couch

Sarah Lincoln is playing the piano in Peoria, trying to remember the stepson she has not seen in over a year.

My stepson is 6 foot 4, thinks Sarah. His legs and arms are disproportionately long. His feet and hands are as large as a giant's. He is awkward, very awkward.

Sarah Lincoln stops playing and lights up her corncob pipe. Yes, she thinks, Abe is a big klutz. He hates to shave. His ears are too long and his hair is so coarse and up-endy a body would think it had never felt the touch of a comb.

Yuck, thinks Mary Todd, looking across the breakfast table at her husband's face. This man looks so common, so disorderly. He is an unkempt, filthy product of Pigeon Creek.

The waiter serves breakfast. "Flapjacks *again?!*" Mary Todd's husband rages.

"I'll tell you, son," Stephen Douglas is saying to a young lawyer as they ride a train over the state of Ohio, "that man is limited in certain areas of—shall we say?—intelligence. . . . By his own account, he attended school less than a year his whole life. You know, I'll bet he never once sat down and read a whole book through." Stephen Douglas spits some phlegm into a spittoon. Through the window of the train he sees Ohio passing by. "And when he went into Congress," Stephen

Douglas continues, "did he ever once use the library? No, sir. He knows nothing of the history of our own country. . . ."

The young lawyer smiles. "As the debates with you proved, Senator," he says.

Stephen Douglas smiles. Another asslicker, he thinks.

Lying on the couch of his office, Lincoln is confronted with names he does not recognize. "Who is Descartes?" he demands. "Who is Thomas Hobbes? Who in tarnation is Malthus and why is he supposed to be so fucking important?"

But he is alone in his office and there is no one to tell him these things.

"Your father is critically ill," Sarah Lincoln writes in a painstaking, arthritic hand. "I am certain he will not last the week. Please come at once."

Lincoln stares at his stepmother's letter. His whole left side twitches and he scratches his nose. My business is such, he thinks, that I can hardly leave now. Besides, I have a bad case of diarrhea.

"Some might say he's a son of a bitch," Stephen Douglas is saying. "But actually he's the son of a bastard."

The young lawyer laughs too heartily. "Is that really so, Senator?"

Stephen Douglas nods. "Nancy Hanks was born out of wedlock. . . . They say the very mention of that fact makes him puke like a newborn babe."

Sarah Lincoln is at her desk, writing again. It is difficult for her. "You are a good stepson, Abe," the words come out on the paper. "But being as you're now the President and the husband of a rich woman, don't you think it's about time you put up a marking on your mother's grave? I have put one up on your father's and it would be nice if both could have them."

Nauseated after another distasteful breakfast of flapjacks, Lincoln lies down for a moment in his bedroom. His big feet spill over the end of the bed. He speculates on just what it is in his own blood that he is transmitting to his grandchildren-to-be.

That night he dreams of a grave with a marking: not his mother's, but Ann Rutledge's. He remembers dry-humping Ann when they were kids. There is a severe thunderstorm and the rains steadily fall on the earth that covers Ann. Lincoln cannot stand the drip-drop-drip-dropping. He awakes with a start.

"What is it?" mumbles Mary Todd, who is awake now too.

"Nothing, dear," Lincoln says. "I was just fretting about the Union. Go back to bed now."

Jerk-off, thinks Mary Todd as she fluffs up her pillow. I married a jerk-off and all he wanted was my money.

Sarah Lincoln thinks of the differences between her stepson and his wife.

She is quick, Sarah thinks. But he is slow.

She is passionate, while he is cold.

She has taste. Abe has none.

No wonder, Sarah thinks, he once ran away before the wedding.

"Yep," says Stephen Douglas in the dining-car of the train, "and Mary Todd took me by the hand and we paraded all over Springfield together just so's she'd make old Abe jealous." Stephen Douglas spears an entire flapjack with his fork and wolfs it down. When he is finished, he says, "That's what did it, you know—his hatred of me. That's what finally gave him enough courage to face marrying her finally. He was afraid I'd get into her pants first."

"That whore's not good enough for you anyway, Senator," says his youthful companion.

Asshole, Stephen Douglas thinks. And then he thinks: Ah, Mary. What a crazy night that was.

In bed, trying to get back to sleep, hearing his wife's dull snoring, Lincoln comes to the inescapable conclusion:

Marriage is death.

Or maybe sex is. One or the other, they're both pretty bad.

Sarah Lincoln finishes reading another letter from her stepson. She takes off her spectacles. Why, thinks Sarah, his writing shows no emotion at all. She rocks in her rocker. No emotion at all. What a cold fish.

"And they say he once raped a fourteen-year-old girl," says Stephen Douglas as the train pulls into Philadelphia.

"Yeah, I heard that story," says the younger man.

You'll believe anything I say, won't you? Stephen Douglas thinks. You're a bigger fool than the President.

Lincoln remains sprawled upon his office couch. He has been there all afternoon.

"Do some work, you're the President," Mary Todd says impatiently.

"Leave me alone," says Lincoln, closing his eyes. "I didn't sleep a wink last night."

Mary Todd just shakes her head. "You'd better not fuck up *this* job the way you did your law practice," she says.

But Lincoln does not listen. Instead, he hums a little tune.

Mary Todd slams the door on her way out to the kitchen.

Sarah Lincoln is sitting in the outhouse. One year, she remembers, Abe lost every case he had. When he had another lawyer helping him, sometimes he'd win one or two, but usually not. The only kind of case he won was when he defended the railroad against some farmer who'd got hit by the train.

Sarah is constipated and so must strain at the stool. Those

were the kind of cases Abe liked, she thinks, especially when the farmer had lost a leg or an arm.

Mary Todd is telling the White House cook not to make flapjacks anymore, that her husband can't stand the sight of them. When the cook looks at her questioningly, Mary just makes a turning motion of her finger pointing at her forehead. The cook understands that the President is a lunatic.

The cook is a Negro man. Mary Todd's husband also finds it hard to stand the sight of Negroes, but he has come to realize that they are necessary to do *some* of the work in this world.

"I once heard about a man who shared a carriage with a Negro," Lincoln tells his son, who is lying next to him on the couch. "He came down with syphilis just like that."

"Daddy, what's slavery?" asks the little boy.

"Don't you worry none about *that,*" says Lincoln, breaking into a yawn. "I wish people wouldn't worry so much about slavery." He yawns again. "*I* sure don't." Another yawn. "It doesn't interest me one little bit."

At the train station in Washington, Mary Todd runs up to Stephen Douglas. They hug each other.

"How's old what's-his-face?" Stephen Douglas asks.

Mary Todd tousles Stephen Douglas' hair. "Same as ever," she sighs.

And the two of them smile at each other conspiratorially.

Hmm, says Lincoln, still flat on his back. Jefferson used this nice phrase: "A house divided . . ."

I think I will appropriate that for my own speech. Thank you kindly, Tom.

"Get me a pencil, somebody!" Lincoln roars.

I don't know why everyone hates Abe so much, thinks Sarah

Lincoln, who is eating some Turkish taffy. She still has all her own teeth.

My stepson's a bit peculiar, she says to herself, but he ain't done nothing.

At dinner Stephen Douglas heartily slaps the President on the back, knowing how much the man hates it. Later he blows cigar smoke in his face, and still later, he and Mary Todd sneak off to Lincoln's bedroom to make love.

"You could at least plant one tree in the garden," Sarah writes her stepson. "Or grow some vegetables. But do *something!*"

After her third orgasm, Mary Todd begins laughing. Stephen Douglas nuzzles her, begins laughing too.

"What is it?" he asks.

"That husband of mine," she says. "Sometimes I think he's already dead and we just haven't gotten around to burying him."

Lincoln is on his office couch, reading another letter from his stepmother. Upstairs his wife is getting laid, and Lincoln does not mind this one bit.

I am going to die, thinks Lincoln on the couch. But in the meantime I can make the most of my life.

Real People

I AM TAKING Arthur Goldberg's photograph.

The distinguished former Secretary of Labor, former Associate Justice of the Supreme Court, former Ambassador to the United Nations, is running for Governor of the State of New York.

Arthur Goldberg is eating a hot dog.

He is at a table with other politicians.

With my Nikon I get a shot of Arthur Goldberg biting into a Nathan's Famous hot dog. Through the lens I can see he is scowling at me. Off to the right a black family is also angry with me for taking their picture without permission.

Then my friend Mark comes over. He holds the camera as Arthur Goldberg goes into the dark, cool night. I walk over to Arthur Goldberg as nonchalantly as possible and Mark snaps our picture.

When it is developed, the photo shows me, the candidate for Governor, a stop sign, and an anonymous man wearing a yarmulke.

Sam Levenson is standing at the corner.

I look him over.

"You're Sam Levenson," I tell him. He smiles.

"You laugh at your own jokes," I tell him. He is still smiling.

"You were poor as a child but overcame it," I say. Sam Levenson's grin grows more fixed.

"You wrote a bestselling book once." He nods.

The DONT WALK sign become a WALK sign.

Sam Levenson crosses the street.

"You're famous!" I yell to him.

There is no response. He just keeps walking.

Governor Rockefeller is riding a bicycle. I have my camera, but it is out of film. I curse myself. I wave to Governor Rockefeller. He does not acknowledge me. I make a face, stick my tongue out. No one seems to notice. I think about all the people who use the word "fucking" as an adjective, particularly my friend Joey. Joey has been known to say, "I'm fucking happy." I tell Joey that Governor Rockefeller is the only person who can really say that. Joey socks me on the chin, a playful sock, but it hurts a little.

Governor Rockefeller bicycles past me. People are following him. It is Earth Day and he is being a good citizen by not polluting the air. Governor Rockefeller is going to beat Arthur Goldberg in the election. Arthur Goldberg cannot ride a bicycle at all.

Ronnie Dyson is lying a few feet away from me. He is wearing a bathing suit and sunglasses. It is Christmastime in Miami Beach, and Ronnie Dyson is performing at the hotel. He is the only black person by the pool. He is reading *Herzog* off and on. I don't think he really understands it. He is only nineteen, the same age as me.

That night I watch him perform in the nightclub. He sings "Aquarius," from the Broadway show *Hair*. He mentions a Robert Downey film he is currently appearing in. He is very gracious and makes jokes about getting so black in the sun. The audience of white people laugh.

On the way out I hear a woman say, "He's pretty good, but he needs more poise."

The next day I tell my uncle, "Ronnie Dyson's pretty good but he needs more poise."

My uncle is not listening.

Abbie Hoffman is on campus. He is on the steps of Boylan Hall. Everyone seems to be laughing at him.

"This place sure is Vanilla University," Abbie Hoffman says. "Where are the black people—on the plantation the college president keeps?"

Everyone is laughing.

"You jerks don't have the slightest idea of how to run a revolution," he tells the crowd. Four students are dead at Kent State University.

The crowd all shake their heads.

"You've got to know the enemy before you fuck 'em!" says Abbie Hoffman.

I look at my chemistry professor, who is standing next to me. "Are you giving grades this semester?" I ask him.

He shakes his head, says something. I cannot hear him because the crowd is cheering Abbie Hoffman.

I am pissing into a urinal in the bathroom of a movie theater. I am thinking about Glenda Jackson. For some reason I look to my right. There is a man next to me, pissing into the next urinal. It is Alan King.

I get excited.

I start to turn toward him, then stop myself before I can wet him.

"Thanks," Alan King says. "More people wet me that way."

Afterwards he gives me his autograph.

Betty Friedan is walking across City Hall Park. She is not wearing a bra. Then I remember that I am not supposed to notice things like that anymore, that is the reason we are all here. Betty Friedan is speaking out against sexism. "Sexism" is a new word. An old lady shouts from the crowd: "Give it to them, Betty baby!"

Everyone looks embarrassed, especially Betty Friedan.

I just take photographs like mad.

One girl calls me a pig.

Congressman Emanuel Celler is speaking. We have invited him to the college. He is eighty years old and can hardly stand up. My friend Mark, who arranged his appearance, has made one mistake. He has given Congressman Celler a podium that has wheels on it. As the Congressman keeps talking, he keeps leaning over more and more and it is obvious that he will soon be at a forty-degree angle to the podium. Everyone tries to be polite and pretends that the Congressman is not leaning farther and farther forward.

I question Emanuel Celler about the war. "Didn't you once say, Mr. Celler," I ask, "that the dogs bark but the caravan marches on? Does that mean that *we're* the dogs?"

Everyone applauds. The audience is with me, against the old Congressman.

Leaning very far forward, Emanuel Celler squints down on me. "Could you repeat the question?" he asks me.

"Never mind!" I shout back. Then Mark steps in and rescues the Congressman before he falls.

I am walking home from the hospital. My grandmother has cancer. I am walking through the park, not looking where I am going. I am worried that my grandmother will die.

A bicycle almost runs me over. "Watch out!" says the lady riding it, but she is not angry. Her voice is soft and her smile is wide.

She is Jacqueline Kennedy Onassis. I realize that ten minutes later.

In the supermarket there is a priest in front of me. I recognize him immediately. He is Bishop Fulton J. Sheen. He carries his groceries out of Gristede's and into the street. I follow him, stay about half a block behind.

At a candy store Bishop Sheen stops for Rolaids. It is there that I catch up to him. We walk to his apartment house. I tell him I am going to be a writer. I lie and say I've read one of his books.

"*Peace of Soul?*" he asks.

I nod. "That must be it."

"If you have talent, you shouldn't waste it," Bishop Sheen tells me. "That's almost a sin."

"I won't," I say. "I can promise you that, I swear." Then I laugh.

Before I know it, Bishop Sheen is gone.

Miami Beach again. The Democrats are nominating McGovern and Eagleton. The New York delegation is having a cocktail party. I try to get near Roger Mudd and listen to what he is telling some fat man. When they see me, they go away. Then I go away.

There is music. Mayor Lindsay is dancing with his wife. He is only a delegate now; his Presidential campaign is long dead.

I tap Mayor Lindsay on the shoulder. "May I cut in?" I ask.

The cameras are rolling, so reluctantly the Mayor has to agree.

I dance with Mary Lindsay. "I hear *Women's Wear Daily* would like to interview you," I say.

"Fat chance," Mrs. Lindsay says.

"Four years ago your husband seconded Agnew here," I tell the mayor's wife.

She steps on my foot and Roger Mudd cuts in.

Beverly Sills is eating a tuna salad.

"Are you Beverly Sills?" I ask her.

"Thank you," she says graciously. She is dressed very demurely.

"I like your singing," I say.

She talks with her food in her mouth. "Everyone says that," she tells me.

"Your brother the gynecologist delivered my baby brother," I say. "It was a pretty easy delivery. My mother decided not to have any more kids. What about you?" I ask her.

Beverly Sills motions to me. She wants to whisper something

in my ear. I move closer to her and bend down a little.

"I'm at a loss for words," Beverly Sills tells me.

John Ashbery is walking down the street. I am coming the other way. There is no way our paths will not cross. He is my first Pulitzer Prize winner.

He is carrying a shopping bag from the Strand Book Store. He smiles at me genially.

"Congratulations on all your awards, Mr. Ashbery," I say to him.

He stops for a moment, tries to remember if he knows me.

"What have you got there?" I ask, pointing to the big book taking up his whole shopping bag.

"A dictionary," he says.

"Oh, which one do you find best?"

John Ashbery's fingers run across his mustache. He chuckles.

"I bet you carry that one around all day," I say, "so you can always think of big words to put in your poems."

"That's pretty good," John Ashbery tells me.

I nod. "Yeah. I guess so."

John Ashbery clears his throat. "I have to go now." He motions ahead.

"What's it like, Mr. Ashbery?"

"What's what like?"

"Being real," I tell him. "I've always wanted to know."

John Ashbery points quickly to the right. "Look!" he shouts. "Barbra Streisand's over there!"

I turn my head. It is just an old lady. I don't bother turning my head back. I know John Ashbery will not be there. No one ever is, in the end.

OBJECTS

In the Lehman Collection

THE POPE IS IN the Lehman Collection. He is admiring a Seurat, a study for the Grande Jatte. The Pope steps back to get perspective. People are staring at him.

"He looks younger on TV," one man whispers to his wife.

"Aah, he's nothing, really," says a young man to his girlfriend, a student at Cooper Union. "Take away his robe and his little hat and what have you got?"

But Dayna is impressed with his elegance, his good looks, his long, sensual fingers. She thinks: This is a Pope with mass appeal.

As the Pope turns to look at a Bonnard, his eyes meet Dayna's . . . seconds pass, a lifetime . . . and he turns toward the painting. But Dayna has felt his glance; she has had her audience.

The boy has a T-shirt on. It says, "Some Men Are More Perfect Than Others." He is thin, with long blond hair, and is holding hands with his girlfriend, a small-breasted brunette in exercise sandals. They walk in unison; neither lingers too long nor moves away too quickly.

They walk up one of the stairways leading to nowhere, a blank wall. He whispers in her ear: "I wish you were Eurasian."

She gives him a sly smile. "I wish you'd *act* Eurasian," she says. And pinches his ass.

They walk down the steps together.

Christopher is jogging through the Grand Gallery. He is up to eleven miles a day already. He is sweating profusely, and his face is contorted with pain. He is coming toward the Ingres portrait again, there people tend to bunch up, he has to be careful to avoid them.

He is traveling very fast. Jogging, he only hears brief snatches of conversation. At that high speed, the Doppler effect is operative. Christopher hears:

". . .no, that was Vuillard . . ."

". . .think of how much money . . ."

". . .the domino theory . . ."

". . .My contractions have started . . ."

". . .The first one to paint Christ as a Jew . . ."

". . .I adore cheap sentiment . . ."

A man with a beard and an earring keeps following Dayna. He brushes up against her, pretending to study a Dürer print.

"Excuse me," Dayna says sarcastically, hoping that it will put him off. But it doesn't work.

He keeps following her. Through all of the Collection he is at her side. Finally he says: "I seem to have a talent for frightening you."

Dayna laughs in his face. "The place for fantasy," she tells him, "is in the bedroom."

She strides toward the exit, wondering if he will follow.

The Speaker of the House is drunk. He does not realize that he is in New York. He flew here yesterday, with his secretary, to attend a $100-a-plate fund-raising dinner. But he has had too much bourbon and branch water, and believes himself in Washington.

"This fella Hirshhorn had pretty good taste," the Speaker says.

His secretary is two steps behind him, shuffling papers around.

They stop at a Hans Memling Annunciation, and the Speaker remembers something. He turns back to his secretary.

"This reminds me," he says. "When is the Wild Horses Protection Bill coming to the floor?"

His secretary looks dumbfounded. "After the Memorial Day recess, I think," she tells him.

"Hmmph," the Speaker says. "There ought to be a few nays on that."

As Christopher jogs through the rooms that were taken from Robert Lehman's Fifty-Seventh Street apartment, he waves to the Matises family, who are driving by in their Winnebago.

The Matises family pronounce their name Matisse; they admire Henri but are not related to him. Dr. Matises is driving; he is a Victorian scholar. He and his wife have three sons; Carlyle, Arnold, and Ruskin.

Mrs. Matises points out the window of the camper to a very fine example of Fauvism. The boys study it dutifully; Carl, the eldest, is taking notes.

The camper passes into the next room, where two hippies are trying to hitch a ride. The dirtier-looking one holds up a sign that says: "Mamaroneck." Dr. Matises drives past them without hesitation.

Russ, the youngest boy, is at the back window of the Winnebago. "Faggots!" he shouts at the hippies.

A man from the Midwest has one of those guided-tour tapes playing as he goes from room to room; the earphone doesn't quite fit and it is making him uncomfortable.

He doesn't notice that they have given him the wrong tape. He is not listening to the museum director telling him about the Collection; instead, he hears the play-by-play for the third game of the 1951 playoffs between the Dodgers and the Giants. The man from the Midwest is not sorry that he rented the tape; it is uncomfortable but even that is helping to heighten his enjoyment of the works of art.

His excitement grows as the game goes into the ninth inning, and he stands before a large Cézanne still-life. Suddenly, Bobby Thomson hits the home run, and there is pandemonium. The announcer, Russ Hodges, goes wild: "The Giants win the pennant! The Giants win the pennant! The Giants win the pennant!" The man from the Midwest is transfixed in a delirium of ecstacy. In a few minutes, he will feel faint.

After resting for a while, the man gives back the tape recorder and earphone at the exit. "This is really a fantastic Collection," he tells the girl at the desk. "But poor Ralph Branca will never be the same."

On the first floor, among the plants, a meeting is going on. It is a meeting of the Lenyin and Lachver Benevolent Association. The purpose of the organization is to provide cemetery plots for the members, most of whom come from the same village in Russia.

The minutes of the last meeting are being read.

"This is a nice place," Mr. Koenig whispers to his neighbor.

"Not bad, not bad," says the man, trying to adjust his bifocals.

The minutes are approved by acclamation.

"You don't think it's magnificent?" Mr. Koenig persists.

"It's not bad," his neighbor says, finally taking off his glasses to wipe them with a handkerchief. "But personally, my brother-in-law's got a condominium in Fort Lauderdale puts this place to shame."

Dayna reenters the Lehman Collection, her sweater tied around her waist to hide the stains. She glances at Christopher as he jogs past a Renoir nude. She looks in vain for the Pope. She is lost in thought, and Dr. Matises has to honk his horn. Dayna does not notice that it has started to rain; most people have umbrellas as they walk around.

Her face gets wet, her hair damp and stringy.

She walks through the rooms, but sees nothing.

In one room there is a Sephardic wedding. The band strikes up, the bride and groom dance. "The hora! The hora!" someone shouts. But Dayna does not hear it.

A black man is stabbed, and falls on top of one of the red velvet chairs, the ones that have worn with age. Dayna is oblivious to it all. She does not even notice the men in undershirts playing bocci.

Suddenly she comes alive; she sees a painting that is unfamiliar to her, in a style that she cannot recognize. It is somehow a very stirring piece of art, but the fact that she cannot identify it annoys her. Apparently it is new to the Collection. Yet now it *is* familiar, as if one of her own dreams. The image strikes a half-forgotten scene out of Dayna's own life; maybe something from her childhood.

Her "MMA" button falls from her blouse; it had been fastened to her collar.

She picks it up, places it back on her collar, and finds herself in front of a large Hans Memling triptych of the Madonna.

The lights in the Lehman Collection flicker on and off. Dayna stares at the Madonna and knows she must leave.

Infant Sorrow

1

"Sometimes it makes me sad . . ." he will begin. Then swallow, then close his eyes, then gather his hands around the cup of diet soda, then look down to the floor and to his Earth Shoes.

"Sometimes it makes me sad that no one has ever loved me."

2

His mother would sit on the side of his bed. She would sit there so often it was beginning to cave in on that end.

"I don't want you to get fat," she'd say softly, a dust rag and a can of Pledge in her hands.

His eyes would be closed. "I've got to bulk up," he would tell her. "All weightlifters have to bulk up first. . . ."

Then his mother would close *her* eyes, but only for a moment. "I don't understand why you're doing this, baby."

His fists, his jaw would tighten. "Because I *have* to," he would say. "Now just leave me alone."

3

Everyone would always call Brian before they'd call him. Not only the friends they had in common, but the friends that had been nominally *his* as well. It had to do with Brian being a nicer person than he was. Brian wasn't as smart or as strong or as quick. But on the other hand, people *liked* Brian.

He saw Brian riding a bicycle with a blonde girl with glasses. He saw them in the rear-view mirror. He stopped the car.

Brian called out his name in surprise.

"It's been years," he said. And even though he knew it was the wrong thing to do, he recited his credentials to Brian: his trophies, his titles, his offers to endorse products. He even went so far as to pull out a certificate of recognition from the back seat of the car.

Brian *was* a nice person. He actually seemed pleased for the other.

Finally he said to Brian, "I don't want to hold you up." He would have liked to wish Brian a good life, but he knew that it wasn't necessary. However, if Brian had wished *him* a good life, he would have felt protected. For the rest of the day at least.

4

When he was very young he was very constipated. Sometimes he did not go to the bathroom for weeks. His grandmother would cry that the boy's appendix must be on fire. They gave him malt-flavored syrup to put in his milk. And raisin bran. And thermometers. And sometimes they would give him glycerin suppositories too.

In the summer people would come into his grandmother's bungalow to watch him straining at the stool. The bathroom door would be open wide and sometimes people would bring their guests for a weekend barbecue. They wanted to see this boy that had trouble going to the bathroom.

He would take his meals on the toilet seat. He would drink ice water or water flavored with Teddy Snowcrop. He would draw pictures of Winky Dink and of Jordan, his stuffed bunny. And he would sweat and strain and say hello to all the people filing past the open bathroom door.

When there was a bowel movement, his grandmother would make a party. It was more for the adults than for him.

5

Working out was his whole life. When he worked out, nothing mattered. He would be on his slant bar lifting the weights, looking at himself in the mirror out of the upper corner of his eye. He would jump rope sometimes until he threw up, but that didn't matter either. It was all there: vascularity, definition, mass, separation. He was making something of himself in a new sense. Pygmalion and Galatea both.

He couldn't understand why he still had trouble falling asleep. Then someone recommended vervain tea. He tried it. It was green and kind of seaweedy, but it seemed to work. At least he got to sleep on time. It didn't prevent him from waking up too early.

6

He watched the news on television all the time. When he drove, his car radio would be turned to an all-news station. Music didn't interest him; there were no words, there was no information there.

He would have dreams about the news, about the President, about civil wars in Beirut and Belfast, about sickening crimes and circus jury trials. He was never a participant in the action of the dreams. No. He was usually a reporter or a cameraman or else a passerby caught in the range of the lens.

7

When something—like meeting Brian or remembering how his grandmother used to cry over him—made him consider his life, he always realized that he was, in the strictest sense, third-rate. And what did it matter that the editors of slick magazines whose offices were in midtown Manhattan took for granted that he was a success? To him it only showed how foolish the world was. When he started seeing the posters of himself in the windows of stores in shopping malls, he wanted to hide. But finally there was too much of him to do that. He had become, as they told him, "too marketable," too valuable a commodity to simply evaporate and be in another place. He had to live inside the body he'd made for himself.

Peninsular People

On the peninsula there is a beach. There is a boardwalk and an amusement park. On the peninsula there is lemon sherbert, and an albino rabbit, and contraband porcelain. On the peninsula there is love.

On the peninsula there is Valerie. Valerie, who used to relax her dates by first sending out her little brother to fight with them; that is, until her brother got too big and too embarrassed, and after that, her dates didn't need relaxing anyway. Valerie, who on occasion would wear a derby. Valerie, who has beautiful breasts. Valerie, whose room was so filled with plants that her boyfriend, when he slept over, would worry about them taking his oxygen away. Valerie, who once gave me a cutting that refused to grow.

On the peninsula there is Mr. Schneider. Mr. Schneider, whose landlord cheats him. Mr. Schneider, who walks with a cane on the boardwalk, glad to have an apartment and not be in a home. Mr. Schneider, who drinks tea from a glass with a lump of sugar between his teeth. Mr. Schneider, who was a tailor, and whose name means "tailor," and who once loved the woman he worked for, a globe-trotting Irish lady, and never said a word.

You can see Mrs. Cramer on the peninsula. Mrs. Cramer, who had a breast removed. Mrs. Cramer, who once took care of six children with chicken pox. Mrs. Cramer, riding her giant tricycle with the big basket for shopping. She is called "eccentric" by Valerie and "crazy-rich" by Mr. Schneider. Mrs. Cramer, who pretended not to know of her husband's only infidelity, and never regretted it.

Daniel is on the peninsula. Daniel, who has been running eleven miles barefoot on the beach every morning. Daniel, who gets depressed otherwise. Daniel, whose stomach muscles are as clean as Alley Oop's. Once he tried, and failed, to get Valerie in the back seat of his brother's Volkswagen. Daniel, who, when I asked, "What do you think about when you run?" answered, "About how good it's going to feel when I stop," and who wasn't joking.

On the peninsula there is Dede. Dede, who, according to her sister-in-law, married the wrong man. Dede, who went out on the beach in a bikini in her eighth month and who later had a brain-damaged child and a divorce. Dede, who appeared in a photograph on the front page of The *Daily News,* wearing her bikini, the polka-dot one, and heading into the surf. The caption read, "The Beaches Were Jammed," and Dede got dozens of phone calls the next day, some of them obscene. Dede, who appeared on a talk-show that week, and who was written up in a whole article. Soon everyone learned that Dede could beat every man but her father in arm-wrestling, and that her terrier was named Holliday, after Judy Holliday, and that she liked all food except butter and anchovies. But no one ever learned of the brain-damaged baby.

And there is Helen, who walks on the beach at midnight with a boy who does not know that she had an abortion at sixteen; and Dede's brother, who does know; and Mrs. Stoner, who has cancer; and Lenny the paper maven, who knows everything there is to know about paper, who has dozens of photographs of his cross-country trips, all of them with funny captions.

The Weitzes, who live on the peninsula, are a five-surfboard family. They are aspiring or failed actors; they are psychology majors turned dancers; they are mountain climbers and real-estate saleswomen and managers of Burger Kings. The Weitzes live above their means. All of them smoke marijuana, and are liberated, and are Unitarians, and are bored.

A widower named Mr. Slutsky watches television all day, mostly game shows and reruns of decade-old comedies. He sits on his terrace and sees the ocean, and he watches other men, sometimes older men, play shuffleboard and handball, and talk. And he is content. Mr. Slutsky, who ran away from home at seventeen, slept on a bench on Houston Street, and found himself in the army in Manila, standing guard over a corporal who had killed a sergeant in a barroom brawl. Mr. Slutsky, who sprained his back when he first lifted his only granddaughter, and who loves her more today because of it. Mr. Slutsky, of the cataracts and diabetes, whose wife, now dead, was introduced to him by Mrs. Stoner, now dying. Mr. Slutsky, who never told his father he loved him, a silent man with a handlebar mustache who invented flying machines and played the violin and corresponded with Zola and planted bombs for the Bolsheviks. Mr. Slutsky, who worries about other people.

There is Mrs. Vincente, who didn't listen to people and refused to put her mother in a home, and her son Louis, who keeps taking the law boards in hopes of scoring better and who is marking time in the meantime. They like living on the peninsula.

Mr. Haring is the father-in-law of Dede's brother. He is bald and an executive for a market-research firm; he drinks much coffee and loves to tend his garden and plays an eager but ultimately incompetent game of tennis. Mr. Haring can do The Hustle. He grew up in London during the war and remembers the Blitz and his school being bombed and a sign amidst the rubble of the school library saying Business As Usual. Mr. Haring works at things.

On the peninsula there is Mrs. Mulcahy, who told me she lived a wasted life. Mrs. Mulcahy, whose husband was a musician, and whose best friend told her about the woman in the front row of the orchestra every night and that something was going on. Mrs. Mulcahy, whose husband showed up late one night with a beautiful pullover sweater, and wouldn't tell her at what store he bought it. Mrs. Mulcahy, who unraveled the sweater and let her husband come home the next night to find two balls of wool atop the fireplace. Mrs. Mulcahy, who divorced her husband, and was bitter, and is bitter to this day.

There is Fat Rosemary, whose boyfriend left her for another girl and who, when Daniel told her, "It's a step down for him," kissed Daniel's cheek and said, "What a dear . . . wonderful . . . *accurate* thing to say."

And Kathy, who refuses to second-guess herself; and Mr. Mudd, who is growing sideburns and once found a bloated body washed up on the sand; and Mike Collangelo, who dreams of plane crashes; and Mrs. Mendez, who wonders what her son could be doing in Italy besides pinching other men's asses.

On the peninsula Mr. and Mrs. Murray live, married fifty-five years and still bickering. If he says it's Sunday, she will say Monday. Mr. Murray, who at seventy-five still gets up at six A.M. to go into work, and Mrs. Murray, who at seventy-three still likes him to sleep only in his V-neck undershirt; his "wee-neck," Mr. Murrays calls it. They were once very rich, but the hospital bills were very big, and now the Murrays make do on the peninsula. If they complain, they don't do it to me.

There is their grandniece Ann-Carol, who plays the dulcimer. Ann-Carol, who is selfish. Ann-Carol, who has the courage to walk down the street holding hands with her lover, another girl. Ann-Carol, who fights with her therapist. Ann-Carol, who was loved by Mr. Haring's son-in-law, Dede's brother; who was loved by one of the Weitzes; who was loved by me.

I am not of the peninsula, but I spend much time there now. There is a bridge you must cross to get there and they are raising the toll and that will discourage bridge traffic. So I will either have to go there less often, or else move there for good. Walking along the beach, on the boardwalk, in the amusement park—there I am happy. Only on the peninsula do I live.

Triptych

ALL PSYCHIATRISTS ARE UNHAPPY.

Dr. Luria is a psychiatrist.

Dr. Luria is unhappy.

The world is a cold, unbeautiful place, says his patient Maria LiMandri.

Dialing.

Maria LiMandri is dialing.

Maria LiMandri is dialing her psychiatrist, Dr. Luria.

Dr. Luria's line is busy.

He is talking to his nephew, Fred Bernstein.

Maria LiMandri is frustrated.

Fred Bernstein is an insurance actuary.

Dr. Luria is bored.

What is Dr. Luria's greatest fear?

That he helps no one get better.

What is Maria LiMandri's greatest fear?

There are two, of equal severity. One is the fear of going on an elevator ride; the other is of dying.

What is Fred Bernstein's greatest fear?

That his tax returns for last year will be audited.

Maria LiMandri is a beautician. There is a mole on her left breast. The mole has a small reddish hair. Dr. Luria imagines that Maria LiMandri has nice breasts. He watches them as Maria LiMandri talks. She is very unhappy.

Dr. Luria has arthritis. One day he will not be able to walk. His nephew Fred Bernstein wonders how he will get along when that day comes. Fred Bernstein tries to imagine Dr. Luria in a wheelchair, and cannot. Maria LiMandri's father walks with a limp.

Fred Bernstein lost his only son. It was an accident. The boy died in an elevator accident. Fred Bernstein's son was crushed to death. Maria LiMandri read about it on page five of the newspaper. Dr. Luria prescribed Triavil 6/10 for Fred Bernstein, so he would be able to function again. Today he is like a new man, Fred Bernstein's boss says.

Maria LiMandri's wristwatch has been broken for days. She is to be late for work again. She eats runny eggs for breakfast, and forgets to take change for the bus. Dr. Luria misses his wife, who is visiting her brother in Tempe, Arizona. Dr. Luria's brother-in-law is Fred Bernstein's father. Dr. Luria has a cook to make his breakfast.

Fred Bernstein's wife is in a state of undress this morning. Her breasts are ripe for plucking, Fred Bernstein does not think. He is busy poring over actuarial charts. Fred Bernstein notes that black females live longer than black males in certain Western nations. Fred Bernstein's wife is dismayed at the lack of attention. She will go to the beauty parlor, to the beauty parlor on the other side of town, to the beauty parlor where Maria LiMandri does not work.

Dr. Luria does not have a patient scheduled for two o'clock. It is his lunch hour. He takes a phone call from Maria LiMandri. She is crying. Maria LiMandri's life is not worth much, she says. Her mother was retarded and was raped by an attendant at a state institution. Today that same attendant, now a senile old man, passes Fred Bernstein's wife on Ruby Street and thinks: What a piece. Dr. Luria tells Maria LiMandri to come in at their usual time.

Maria LiMandri is compulsive. She cannot go to the bathroom without flushing the toilet three times. Fred Bernstein's boss says he does three times the work of any man in his office. Dr. Luria failed his road test three times before he passed. Now his legs are too weak to drive. It is the arthritis.

Shingles. Under a pile of actuarial charts, Fred Bernstein wonders if he has a case of shingles. On Schermerhorn Street, a shingle falls on the spot where Maria LiMandri's father stood not half an hour before. Were time pushed back an hour, her father might be dead or dying. It would make no difference to Maria LiMandri, as she has never met the man.

Four o'clock in the afternoon. Maria LiMandri has a session with Dr. Luria. Dr. Luria does not begin by saying, "How are you doing now, Maria?" Maria LiMandri does not tell Dr. Luria that she wishes he could adopt her. Fred Bernstein does not interrupt their session with a phone call to say that Dr. Luria's wife has died in Tempe, Arizona, while visiting her brother, Fred Bernstein's father. Everything is proceeding according to plan.

What does Dr. Luria have for supper?

Shell steak, medium rare; Brussels sprouts; creamed corn; a glass of Lancer's rosé wine; a cup of Darjeeling tea; and a pain-killer.

What does Maria LiMandri have for supper?

A cheeseburger and a coke.

What does Fred Bernstein have for supper?

Hearts of lettuce; onion soup; corned beef and cabbage; seltzer water; two pieces of strawberry cheesecake; a chocolate bar.

Of the three, only Fred Bernstein gets indigestion.
Maria LiMandri's bowel movements are normal.
Dr. Luria is forever constipated, a side effect of pain-killers.

It is becoming evening. Fred Bernstein is going to bed with his wife. She is fantasizing about her hairdresser's strong hands and the peacock tattoo on his arm. Fred Bernstein's wife's hairdresser once smiled at Maria LiMandri on a crowded crosstown bus. Neither knew they were in the same profession.

Dr. Luria is in bed, watching a game show while reading a medical journal. The pain-killers are making him sleepy.

Maria LiMandri is in her bed as well. She is trying to think of the Italian word for "lovelorn," as in "advice to the lovelorn."

In what order do they fall asleep and how do their dreams bring them closer together?

Dr. Luria falls asleep first, followed three-quarters of an hour later by Maria LiMandri. Fred Bernstein cannot sleep because of indigestion and worry. His wife is snoring. Fred Bernstein's face appears in Maria LiMandri's first dream of the night, but she does not know who he is and so ignores him. Dr. Luria dreams of Maria LiMandri sucking his genitals aboard a boat steaming down a mosquito-infested African river. This is Dr. Luria's third dream of the night. Fred Bernstein still cannot sleep. Maria LiMandri is well into her third dream, which features tigers and canny hypnotists who turn out to be fathers of little girls. Dr. Luria dreams for his fifth dream a dream of Fred Bernstein's wife killing her husband and burying different parts of Fred Bernstein's body in each of the fifty states. Fred Bernstein instinctively knows he is being dreamed about, and to ward off death, he finally falls asleep. Within two hours he is dreaming of his dead son. At this point Maria LiMandri wakes up in a cold sweat. She knows that Dr. Luria, her psychiatrist, has died of a cerebral hemorrhage. Unhappily, Dr. Luria just sleeps.

Classified Personal

LONESOME POPULAR: I'm male, 23, into rock, wheels, pinball. From So. Jersey, shy, lacking the confidence necessary to walk up to a strange girl and say "Hey toots! What are you doing for the rest of your life?" Wide variety of interests and musical tastes ranging from soft to hard rock all the way out to space. Looking for a relationship with a future? Please call me (609) 781-9980 after 5 p.m. Ask if this is a Quiet Zone, I'll have a snappy answer by then. QUIET ZONE

To W/F 18–21: I'm W/M, 19, 6′2″, slim, average looks. I've had it with this damn materialistic plastic society. Looking to escape in mind and spirit by finding someone who truly cares. Deeply into nature (camping, long walks, sunsets), music (Tull, C. Stevens, M. Blues). I'm a loner who doesn't hang out with a crowd. Not looking for just another relationship. Looking for one who has been screwed up and is in need of an honest, sincere relationship. So if you're not materialistic and need someone to lean on like I do, write COUGAR.

DASHING DOM DIGS DAINTY DRAG DOLLS. Bi/M desires femme TV and fi queens from 21–30, but all answered. Seeks sensuous, sexy, slim, shaven, bra and bikini, bathing beauty "babes." A queen who will tease and then please in mutual frenchship and other delicious delights. Prefer leggy, lovely "ladies" on hormones and with own pad, but all answered. Amateur or pro OK, any marital status OK, wife participating OK, any area of N.Y., N.J., Pa. OK—all answered. Write DOM, P.O. Box 467, Lakewood, N.J. 07968. Phone/photo answered first.

Reply to CHELSEA: I'm a 20 yr. old who looks 15 or 16, 5′7″, 130, black hair, brown eyes, into same and agree. In need of someone who feels the way you do. DREAM MERCHANT

To the boy in pain: I can't do much. I can't take it away. I can only let you know that I have and still do feel it, and at moments feel it so strongly in you. Ask for anything you need and you know you have it. I'm not scared anymore. All my love.

Mrs. Robinson, where are you? Please teach me how. W/M, considered goodlooking, shy, but I'm slowly falling apart. Please reply with a way of contacting you. THE IMPOTENT KID

SAPPHO: I'd like to correspond. To do so sooner, go to round building bathroom on first floor by Student Union. Leave message on wall in last cubicle on right. What is your major? Are you a dorm student or commuter? Reply to LESLIE in bathroom soon.

W/F, 19, blonde, attractive, alone in USA, hooked on everything bad. Seeks older man, 20–30, for help before I hit bottom. If anyone cares, reply to HELGA with way to contact.

Rowena, Rowena: The first time should be extra special. I can help you. CAPTAIN MIDNITE

HANDICAPPED FEMALES, any age. W/M, 26, wounded in Nam, understands your feelings. Will satisfy every desire and fantasy no matter what you are into. I am sincere. D.F.

DENNY: I am a W/Bi/M, 15, and very lonely. I dig older, stronger, tough guys like you. I am good looking, blonde and live on Staten Island. Let's please meet in Staten Island

10/21/75 at 4 p.m. in front of mall. Hope to see you. ADMIRER

I'm a W/M, 19, looking for a W/F 16–19, for a lasting relationship. I've been writing ads for months with no luck. Please help. One person is all I need, but I need her now. Loneliness is awful. Reply to WATCHING AND WAITING.

I'm an 18 yr. old male and I just finished reading the personals. My head got so blown apart from them. Is there any for real, together, straight females out there, 18–20? BLOWN HEAD

BOY NEXT DOOR: Straight-appearing athletic dude with dirty blond hair, blue eyes, boyish good looks, seeks boy of my dreams. Similar handsome H.S./College jock/stud. All-American type who really fills a pair of Levis. Need close buddy. Letter/photo to Box 21, Teaneck, N.J. 09712

Are there any guys out there whose main interest isn't just getting laid? Sex is fine, if there's the right understanding behind it. Do you exist, a W/M, 18–25? I like sincere people, good times. I am a W/F, 18. Reply to MYSTERY LADY

JOHN WITH 4-DOOR BLUE SEDAN: Was to meet you in front of movie on Tues. Couldn't make it as I bowl. Make new date. Try another night.

This brother's in the pen for a dope beef. Sure could handle some loving words from some foxy ladies. If you're "right," hurry up and get down with some words and flicks. DWAYNE 27580 P.O. Box 450 Jefferson City, Mo. 65893

W/F, 23, diehard folkie, wishes to befriend male, 23–27, who is insightful, articulate, discriminating, musical and crazy. I feel as though I'm an anachronism. Do you? Reply (it's karmic, anyway, if you do) to COUSIN CATERPILLAR

Adorable feminine bi girl wishes to meet same for lots of fun. No libbers or wrestlers. ROSIE

W/M, 22, very boyish looking, would love to be "educated" and "disciplined" in the ways of sex by a very dynamic and aggressive girl ages 17–22. I am very shy and remain a virgin. I would do anything a girl would ask. Respond to SEX STUDENT in next issue.

To Paul B: You're a really groovy far-out dude, man. You can bang my keys anytime, anywhere, anyplace. Look out 'cause I'm watching you. Signed—TAKE ME I'M YOURS. P.S.—This is not your chick.

Boy, very handsome, blond, blue eyes, 5′11″, 140 lbs. Just turned 18. Like basketball, skiing, surfing and grass. Want to meet guys who like chicken. Especially somebody with a Corvette. Can meet after school. JIMMY

Reply to JUST MYSELF: A brilliant observation, but do you think for one moment that someone would answer the ad of a person who is short, fat, ugly, has acne and bad breath and the IQ of your average squirrel? Face it, honey, this is a meat market and when selling meat you've got to lie a little and dress up the package! JUST ME, TOO

Reply to Mr. and Mrs. J: Thanks. Will meet you both Monday, January 23 in front of A & P on Route 89 at 7:45 p.m. SLAVE TRADER

Where have all the longhairs gone? Long hair on men is incredibly sexy and beautiful, yet today most men insist on wearing it short. A man without hair is about as appealing as a man without a penis. RAPUNZEL THE PHILOSOPHER

To TIRED OF BEING HURT: I'm a W/F, 18, who loves—absolutely adores—The Eagles. Springsteen is great, too! You appeal to me as a warm human being who wants to share that warmth. Come and be a part of a friendship that can stand up against the cruel stabs of the world. Reply to YOU'LL NEVER CRY

Reply to JIMMY—W/M, 25, good looking, have similar interests, skiing, grass. Love chicken meat. Excited about meeting you. Am discreet and sincere. Let's arrange a date. Friday's the best day. I drive a T-Bird. Contact COLONEL SANDERS

SNOW WHITE: W/M, 17, name is Bob from Rutherford. I don't treat girls like shit. I mean, that is fucked-up. Well, I'm into Kiss, astrology. I'm a Gemini. I'd like to hear from you soon. And if we don't get it on, have a good year.

Greetings and Salutations, Women! It's difficult to sit here and write to ask for something so necessary, yet so very personal. W/M, 21, nice shape, looking for female companionship. Must be into music, life, good times for the sake of good times. Must be free—free in spirit, thought, and desire. If by some slim chance you are a good-looking member of the earth signs, all the better. Respond next issue to Taurus.

HELP!!! I'm a guy trapped in a girl's body! I intend to change surgically. I need friends with the same problems who can accept me for what I am. Please respond. Thanks. LOOKIN' FOR AN ECHO

Darlene—I love you more than bakery cookies!!!!! Am yours, Love, Michael.

NASHVILLE PUSSYCAT: You seem as sweet as fritters and as warm as Tootsie's hominy grits. Let's ride the fences and get to know your southern parts. TEENAGE TARZAN

I'm tired of money-hungry girls who don't believe in mutual respect. If you're a W/F, 16–20, and you enjoy bike riding, long talks, cozy fires and good times, write me. No gays, fems, uglies, fats or airheads. Reply to POSSIBLY THE ONLY STRAIGHT ONE LEFT

Love! Love! Love! Who's got it to give? Lonely, love-starved W/M, 21, affectionate, handsome, muscular and understanding seeks guy with boyish good looks and smooth body for lasting relationship. Write OCCUPANT, Box 44, Carteret, N.J. 07915

Reply to GEMINI: Where you from, you sexy thing? Must meet you. Like bowling, disco, dining out. Am a 25 year old woman, attractive, and financially well off. Baby, I'm rich. Love socializing and social drinking. Let's socialize under some satin sheets. Reply to me, BLACK IS BEAUTIFUL AND DON'T FORGET IT YOU HONKY

Does your name begin with an R? Are you a Cancer or born near Christmas? Do you work in white or are you involved with medicine? Urgent you reply to DENNIS

Howdy! I got the itch between my legs. Looking for one supermama ready, willing and able to satisfy my every desire. Available 12–1 p.m. Fridays. Meet in front of Salem Theatre. Carry an American flag. I'll know it's you. THE RAMROD

I'm tired of this bullshit. I've been alive for almost 20 years just yearning to give my love to someone but have constantly been screwed. I just can't stand playing games any longer. I loved one person in my life who didn't give a damn about me. I never thought that living could be so empty, but without the love of a beautiful woman, life just isn't worth living. If you're a tall, slim, attractive female who is interested in honestly loving someone, I think that you should help me. I have so much to give. There is so much I want to do with a natural girl who realizes that feelings are not things to be played with. This is the last ad I plan on placing so I'd like to thank this paper for giving people like me an outlet for expression. Life without true and total love is not life. If I don't find someone this time, I'll just end it all anyway. I know I'm lost and I know a loving and caring and beautiful woman is my only way out to happiness. POTENTIAL SUICIDE

FAMILIES

Wednesday Night At Our House

How many people live in our house?
Five.

What are their names and ages?
David, 50; Michelle, 45; Robert, 25; Eliot, 23; Jeffrey, 15.

What are they doing now?
Jeffrey is lifting a ninety-pound barbell above his head for ten repetitions six times each; Eliot is lying in bed talking to his girlfriend on one telephone; Robert is reading *Circus Magazine* and looking at a photograph of Andy Gibb; Michelle is putting a head of lettuce in a Tupperware container; David is chain-smoking and yelling at his mother on the other telephone.

Why is David yelling at his mother?
Because she says she could not visit David's father at the nursing home today in Florida.

What is the matter with David's father?

He had a stroke and is now a vegetable.

What does David's mother say about David's father?

That he brought on the stroke himself; that he didn't know how to live; that now he doesn't know how to die; that he could have had a few years left; that she sees men in their eighties enjoying themselves all over the condominium where she lives; that it was her bad luck to be married to David's father for fifty-seven years.

What does David tell her?

That she has to accept that her husband is not going to get any better; that she should stop comparing herself to other people; that if she is going to die, she better come back north so at least she'll have family around; that otherwise she better learn to live by herself; that she should take care of her own health.

How does David's mother respond to this?

By saying, "If only he hadn't gone to play pinochle that day. . . ." By saying, "If only he'd learn how to control his bowels, I could take him home. . . ." By saying, "If only he took care of himself he could have had a few good years left. . . ." By crying.

What does David warn his mother not to do?

David tells her not to drive his father's 1971 Buick Century, or at least to drive it only to the Skyland Shopping Mall once a day and no more.

Why does he say this?

Because David's mother has had arthritis for many years and has not driven a car since 1971; because she is going deaf and getting senile; because David fears she will kill herself or other residents of North Miami Beach.

Who does David's mother curse?
Her daughter Rose, David's only sister.

Why does David's mother curse Rose?
Because Rose was no help to her when she came down to Florida; because Rose left Florida and is not there now; because she has always abused Rose.

Why doesn't David ask his mother how his father is?
Because his father is always the same, having some bad days when he breaks other patients' radios and tears the bedsheets, having some good days when he recognizes people and remembers the names of all of his grandchildren and great-grandchildren.

What does David's mother feel toward David's father?
Anger—because she must live alone now. Envy—because he does not know what is going on and she does. Hate—because he ruined her life. Love—because she was his wife for fifty-seven years. Guilt—because when *she* was dying, her husband spent hundreds of thousands of dollars to save her and because he spent days and nights by her bedside until he was certain she was not going to die.

How does David's mother express her guilt to David?
By saying, "If it were me in that nursing home, he'd be there every day." By saying, "If it were me who was sick, he would have found a way to keep me in Villa Maria."

What is Villa Maria?

The finest nursing home in all of the state of Florida. Three years ago when David's mother broke her arm, she stayed at Villa Maria and received the best care in the world. Two months ago, when David's father had his stroke and was released from the hospital, he stayed at Villa Maria but they couldn't keep him there.

Why couldn't they keep David's father at Villa Maria?

Because they only take a certain percentage of Medicare patients; because David's father was reevaluated and they decided therapy could not help him; because David and Rose and their mother could not afford to pay for Villa Maria without Medicare; because they couldn't expect Villa Maria to throw out their Medicare patients who were already there to make room for a newcomer.

Besides the good care, what was so good about Villa Maria?

Another man in the condominum had a wife there and he visited her every day. He could have given David's mother a ride to see her husband every day. Now she can only go once a week or so to the new nursing home.

What did David and his mother do to try to keep David's father at Villa Maria?

They pleaded for forty-five minutes with the Director. They cried.

What did the Director say after they pleaded and cried?

He said nothing. He sighed. He picked up the phone, pushed a button and asked the Head of Admissions to come to his office.

What did David think was going to happen then?

David thought that they would make an exception in his father's case.

What did the Director of Villa Maria say when the Head of Admissions came into the office?

"Will you please try to get Mr. Schwartz into a different nursing home?"

What was David's reaction when he heard this?

Rage. Impotence. Terror.

What is David's reaction now when he thinks of this incident as he talks to his mother?

Guilt—because she is implying that David's father could have kept *her* in Villa Maria if she were ill; because she is implying that David is not doing all he can for his father.

What does David do when he hangs up the phone?

Sits on his wife's night table. Finishes his third Winston. Belches. Looks at his wife and sons who have come into the room asking him who he was yelling at.

What do the five people do next?

They talk about death and how much better it would be if David's father had died. Michelle says this is only because David's father was such an active man. Robert says he talked to David's father only two days before the stroke and he sounded fine. Eliot says that David's father is comfortable now, like a retarded person who does not know any better. Jeffrey says nothing and goes into his and Eliot's room to read the Bible.

Why does Jeffrey read the Bible?

Because he believes in every word of the Old Testament. Because he has become an Orthodox Jew. Because it is a minor Jewish holiday and he is not permitted to watch television.

Who makes up the rules of what Jeffrey is permitted and not permitted to do?

Jeffrey does.

What are Jeffrey's only concerns?

Bodybuilding: observing Orthodox Judaism; television.

What do the other people in the family think of Jeffrey?

David thinks he may be a little peculiar but at least he's not taking drugs. Michelle thinks he may be a little peculiar but at least he's not a Jesus freak. Robert thinks that Jeffrey is a compulsive neurotic with great guilt feelings and possible agoraphobia. Eliot says that Jeffrey's sickness is expanding from his brain and filling up the air in the room that they share and poisoning it.

What does Robert say when he hears what Eliot says about Jeffrey?

"I trust you're speaking metaphorically."

What does Michelle say when she hears what Eliot says about Jeffrey?

"You've got to understand that there are reasons for certain rituals in his religion. Millions of people—well, thousands, anyway—think the way he does. He's just practicing what he believes."

What does David say when he hears what Eliot says about Jeffrey?

"Just try to accept him and his beliefs. You may think they're crazy and your mother may think they're crazy and Robert may think they're crazy and *I* may think they're crazy. . . . But there are worse things he could be doing."

What does Jeffrey say when he hears what Eliot has said about him?

Nothing. He is too busy reading the Bible and muscle magazines.

What does Eliot do to calm himself?

He puts on a Yes album very loud. He puts the pillow over his head. He takes off his shirt. He calls his girlfriend on the telephone.

What are Robert and David trying to do?

They are trying to fill out a Medicaid form for David's father.

How do David and Robert react while filling out the form?

David gets agitated and smokes two Winstons. Robert remains calm and says, "Dad, you can't let these pieces of paper intimidate you."

Why do pieces of paper intimidate David and not Robert?

Because David is more honest than his son. Because David is older than his son. Because David remembers when pieces of paper could destroy a person's life and his son does not.

Are there any pieces of paper that could destroy Robert's life?

Probably not. But there might be.

What might these pieces of paper be?

Robert's CIA file, containing photographs of him at various SDS demonstrations during the years 1969–1971, containing articles he wrote for his column in his undergraduate newspaper in which he spelled America *Amerika,* containing testimony he gave before his college's student-faculty disciplinary committee concerning a riot following the appearance of a Navy recruiter on campus.

Is Robert a radical?

He was. Now he is a moderate.

Is David a moderate?

He was. Now he is a conservative.

Are Robert, David, Michelle and Eliot members of any organized political group?

Yes. They are all members of the Democratic party.

Did Robert, David, Michelle and Eliot vote in the 1977 Democratic primary for Mayor of New York City?

Robert, David and Michelle did. Eliot did not because he and his girlfriend were in Pennsylvania Dutch country at the time and because Eliot feels that all politicians are worthless.

Who did Robert, David and Michelle vote for in the Mayoral primary and why?

They all voted for losing candidates. David voted for Mayor Beame because he sympathized with the Mayor's problems and because the Mayor reminded him of his father and because the Mayor, David felt, did the best he could under difficult circumstances. Michelle voted for Bella Abzug because she is a woman and has a big mouth and could probably straighten things out just by scaring people. Robert voted for Herman Badillo because he figured that Herman Badillo had no chance of getting elected, was the most intelligent candidate, and probably could use an extra vote since no one but Puerto Ricans would vote for him.

Why do Robert, Eliot, Jeffrey, David and Michelle continue to live in New York City?

Robert continues to live there because it is the cultural capital of the world and because he has a teaching job there. Eliot continues to live there because his girlfriend lives there. Jeffrey continues to live there because he is only fifteen and must stay with his parents. David continues to live there because he is in business there. Michelle continues to live there because David is in business there.

Where would they rather live?

David and Michelle would rather live just outside Fort Lauderdale, Florida. Jeffrey would rather live in Port-au-Prince, Haiti. Eliot would rather live in Santa Monica, California, or Boulder, Colorado. Robert would not rather live anywhere except perhaps part of the summer in Manchester, Vermont.

What is the general state of their health?

David smokes too much, has high blood pressure and a 435 cholesterol count. Michelle is thirty pounds overweight, has varicose veins and dysmenorrhea. Robert has acne vulgaris and ingrown toenails but is generally healthy. Eliot is allergic to twenty-seven different substances, is often short of breath, suffers from terrible sinusitis, has never fully recovered from pneumonia and mononucleosis, and is generally unhealthy. Jeffrey gets frequent sore throats.

How much money do they have?

David and Michelle have several joint bank accounts, own forty-one shares of common stock, David's parents' condominium in Florida, three cars, their home, and have an estimated net worth of $737,900. Robert has seven shares of stock, fourteen U.S. savings bonds, a small savings account, a small checking account, and has an estimated net worth of $3,100. Eliot has twenty shares of stock, seven pounds of marijuana in his drawer, a stereo, a savings account, and has an estimated net worth of $5,600. Jeffrey has an estimated net worth of $212, all from a savings account and U.S. savings bonds.

How do they earn their money?

David imports jeans from South Korea and sells them at a profit. Michelle gets an allowance from David. Robert teaches part-time at a university. Eliot collects unemployment insurance and sells marijuana. Jeffrey gets an allowance from David and gifts from his grandparents.

What are their favorite foods?

David: pickled onions. Michelle: all vegetables except broccoli. Robert: hamburgers. Eliot: chocolate layer cake. Jeffrey: cottage cheese with crabapple jelly.

What are their favorite movies?

David: "Our Town." Michelle: "Gone with the Wind." Robert: "The Discreet Charm of the Bourgeoisie." Eliot: "A Clockwork Orange." Jeffrey: "The Loneliness of the Long Distance Runner."

What are their favorite TV shows?

David: "Monday Night Football." Michelle: "Family." Robert: "All My Children." Eliot: "Saturday Night Live." Jeffrey: "The Gong Show" and "The Stanley Siegel Show."

Who are their favorite authors?

David: Vladimir Nabokov. Michelle: Saul Bellow. Robert: D. H. Lawrence and John Galsworthy. Eliot: Irving Wallace. Jeffrey: the writers of the Old Testament.

What birds do they most resemble?

David: ostrich. Michelle: flamingo. Robert: sparrow. Eliot: blue jay. Jeffrey: penguin.

Which other member of the family do they love the most?

David: Michelle. Michelle: David. Robert: David. Eliot: Michelle. Jeffrey: Eliot.

Ten years ago, which other member of the family did they love the most?

David: Michelle. Michelle: Jeffrey. Robert: Michelle. Eliot: Jeffrey. Jeffrey: Michelle.

Which of them hates Wednesday nights the most?

Michelle, because she knows the cleaning woman will not be coming in the next day, Thursday.

Which of them hates Wednesday nights the least?

Robert, because he does not have to work the next day.

Who is the strongest member of the family emotionally?

David thinks that Robert is. Michelle thinks that she is. Robert thinks that he is. Eliot thinks that David is. Jeffrey thinks that no one in the family is strong emotionally.

On this Wednesday night, how do they deal with the fact that they will all die?

David tries not to think about it. Michelle wishes David would write a will. Robert repeats to himself before going to bed, "Anyone can die at any time." Eliot smokes marijuana in his car. Jeffrey prays to God.

How do they think they will die?

David thinks he will have a heart attack. Michelle thinks she will die of old age. Robert thinks he will commit suicide. Eliot thinks he will die in an auto accident. Jeffrey thinks that he will get cancer.

What will happen when David's father dies in the morning?

David will fly down to Florida and bring his mother and his father's body back to New York for the funeral. He will sit *shiva* and go through a long period of depression, cry at odd moments, develop psychosomatic symptoms and eventually become a stronger person. Michelle will cry as she remembers the last time she saw her father-in-law, when he told her that he loved her like a daughter and she couldn't tell him that she loved him. She will get closer to her own father. Robert will not cry but will take to his bed for two days. At the funeral he will recite Dylan Thomas's "Do Not Go Gentle into That Good Night." Eliot will cry and rationalize the death, saying his grandfather was an old man. Eliot's girlfriend will comfort him. Jeffrey will continue to lift weights and read the Bible, secure in the knowledge that his grandfather has gone to a better world.

Slowly, Slowly in the Wind

HERE WE GO AGAIN. Grandpa and Grandma have taken the newspaper coupons and the shopping cart and gone out to Pantry Pride. I am in the apartment, watching Great-Grandma Chaikah. She is watching Dinah Shore.

"You know she's Jewish?" Great-Grandma Chaikah says. "Southern but Jewish."

I nod. The bell rings.

It is Mrs. Brody, our neighbor. She has just gotten back from Fort Lauderdale. She brings us a bag of oranges. Mrs. Brody tells me to brush my teeth after I eat the oranges, the acid is bad for the enamel. "Then you'll be stuck one day with dentures," Mrs. Brody says.

Great-Grandma Chaikah stops watching Dinah Shore. She starts watching Mrs. Brody.

"How many children you got?" Great-Grandma Chaikah asks her. "Myself, I got five, twelve grandchildren, three greats. He's one of the greats," she says, pointing to me.

"I got two sons," Mrs. Brody says. "One's a doctor."

"Very nice," sighs Great-Grandma Chaikah. "And the other son?"

"Oh, he's in Medicine now."

"You mean he's a doctor too?"

"No, he *lives* in Medicine. Medicine, Wisconsin."

Great-Grandma Chaikah turns her back on Mrs. Brody, goes back to watching Dinah Shore.

I begin to eat an orange.

"Surprise!" Grandma says when she and Grandpa get home. "We went to McDonald's. Quarter-Pounders for everybody tonight!"

"Except me," Grandpa puts in. "I get a Filet-o-Fish. I've got to watch my cholesterol."

"Mine better be with cheese," Great-Grandma Chaikah says. Dinah Shore is saying goodbye to her.

We put away the groceries, prepare the dinner table.

"The girl at the counter made a mistake," Grandma tells us proudly. "Charged us ten cents less on Temp-tee Cream Cheese." Sometimes Grandma peels off the price labels on groceries till she gets to a price she likes. She is a good shopper.

On TV, they have a teaser for "Eyewitness News." "Eight-year-old son of a rabbi thrown off a roof by a night watchman," Roger Grimsby tells us. "Details coming up."

"How come they say *son of a rabbi?*" Great-Grandma Chaikah wants to know. "If Buddy here got thrown off a roof, they wouldn't say *son of a pants man.*"

"He's a rabbi," Grandpa says with authority. "They got to give him the honor."

"Besides," Grandma says, placing the stringy french fries in a big bowl, "how would it look to say, 'Son of a *priest* gets thrown off a roof?' " And we all laugh and dig into our hamburgers. Great-Grandma Chaikah has to scrape the salt off her french fries because her pressure is very high. Grandma has to drink Sugar-Free Seven-Up because of her diabetes. She is worried about the forthcoming ban on saccharin.

"It's criminal, that's what it is!" she says. "They don't take away his cigarettes!" She means Grandpa, who takes that moment to begin a coughing fit.

"No meal is complete without that man turning purple," Great-Grandma Chaikah whispers in my ear. Grandpa is her oldest son.

We watch Farrah Fawcett-Majors trying to sell us a car.

"Don't you think she's got a foreign accent?" Grandpa asks. Nobody answers him. We are all eating our junk food.

Another teaser for the news: "Coming up next: A building crane falls and kills a little girl . . ."

"Oh, look," Great-Grandma Chaikah says, "That's the one they didn't show last night at eleven."

"They didn't have the film then," I put in.

"Sure," Grandpa says. "What do you think, they can just get it in a minute? It's not an easy business."

Storm Field does the weather. His father is the weatherman on a different channel.

"Eighty-one in Miami today," Grandma says enviously. She is looking at the weather map.

Grandpa, who does not like all the running around people do in Florida, changes the subject. "See, Buddy," he tells me, pointing to Storm Field. "There's a guy with a good job. Someday he'll be bigger than his father."

"You starting in already?" Great-Grandma Chaikah says. "For God's sakes, leave the boy alone."

I am twenty-three years old.

After the local news, I want to watch Walter Cronkite. I want to know what's going on in the world. But we watch "Bowling for Dollars" instead. The first lady up gets the five-ten split.

"She doesn't have any power," Grandma says.

"*I* could do better than that," Great-Grandma Chaikah puts in.

Grandpa says shh. He lights another Pall Mall. "Do you know

that only two Jewish people made two strikes on this show? I don't know what's wrong with them," he tells us.

Not knowing whom he's referring to, the rest of us keep quiet. Great-Grandma Chaikah lets out some gas. "Excuse me," she says.

We all fall asleep watching television. In the middle of the night Great-Grandma Chaikah shakes me awake. Grandma and Grandpa have fallen asleep together on the couch. Grandma's head is on Grandpa's lap. "Isn't that cute," Great-Grandma Chaikah says. "Just like children."

Great-Grandma Chaikah and I go into the next room. She has insomnia and wants me to keep her company. We play kaluki for awhile. I yawn a lot.

She tells me about her husband, my great-grandfather. He died in 1942. "Just a month after Pearl Harbor," she says.

Great-Grandpa was an atheist. He refused to let religion into his house. "That's why your grandfather is so ignorant about everything Jewish. My husband, may he rest in peace, wouldn't let any of the boys be bar-mitzvahed." Then she smiles. "*You* had a nice bar mitzvah," she tells me. "A wonderful affair."

I feel a stirring somewhere in my body. In the back of my mind I am thinking of a girl I know. She is married now, though. She and her husband live in Medicine, Wisconsin.

"When your great-grandfather was dying, for some reason he asked to see a rabbi. So we figured, with him being an atheist, he'd want a Reformed rabbi. He always said he didn't believe in God, he believed in man. Well, he read too much anyways.

"But he insisted on an Orthodox rabbi. Not even a Conservative would suit him. When I asked him why, he said, 'Look, Chaikah, if I'm going to have one, it might as well be the *genuine article.*'

"How do you like that, Buddy?" Great-Grandma Chaikah asks me.

I do not answer my great-grandmother. I am looking out the window, watching the black ocean waves roll in, thinking of other things. She seems to sense this and gets up and goes into the bathroom.

I look at my wristwatch. In six hours it will be a new morning.

On the Boardwalk

I AM WALKING on the boardwalk, trying to watch the breezes blow. Weeks ago some drunken teenagers went on a rampage and destroyed almost all of the benches on the boardwalk. The city cannot afford to put up new benches.

On one of the few benches left standing, my maternal grandparents and my great-uncle are sitting. I go over to them.

They are glad to see me.

Grandma has a herpes blister that's giving her trouble. She keeps touching it. Grandpa is wearing his slippers. Uncle Seymour says he has a riddle to tell me. Go ahead, I say to him.

"A man and his son are driving in a car . . ." Uncle Seymour begins.

I interrupt him. "The doctor was the boy's *mother,*" I say.

"I got another one," Uncle Seymour says.

Uncle Seymour is always with Aunt Pearl unless they are having another fight. I ask Uncle Seymour where Aunt Pearl is.

"She's cooking," he says.

"Usually, when they have a fight, he tells people she's sick," Grandma says. "Then two weeks later, they're still having the same fight, he meets the same person. What does he tell them? 'She's sick.' How long can a person be sick?"

"How long can a person fight?" Grandpa says.

Uncle Seymour stares at the ocean.

Bernard Bergman, the corrupt nursing-home czar, receives a four-month jail sentence. Uncle Seymour is incensed. Bergman is a rabbi, he says, and it will make the whole Jewish race look bad.

"How can we face our Gentile friends?" Grandma says.

"Imagine, a rabbi cheating senior citizens like that," says Uncle Seymour. "They should take away the man's yarmulke."

Grandpa, an atheist, tells about an old rabbi in the forties, a distinguished man, who would order religious books from Jerusalem in what was then Palestine. "It turned out that he was smuggling cocaine in the bindings," Grandpa tells us. "And that was thirty years ago, before any of this." Grandpa makes a sweeping gesture, but we don't know what he is referring to.

"I'd like to write a letter to that judge who let him off so easy," says Uncle Seymour angrily. "I'd give him a piece of my mind. Except I'd be scared to sign my name. All the big shots, they're all corrupt. They could take revenge and stop my social security."

How did Uncle Seymour's fight with Aunt Pearl start? I wonder.

"It's on account of pornography," Uncle Seymour tells me. "Today everything's so free, it's ridiculous." He points at the beach. "Things keep going the way they are, in ten years they'll be bathing in the nude here."

"They do it now," Grandpa informs him. "Only not here yet. But they do it in Europe and on Fire Island."

Grandma looks away, embarrassed.

Uncle Seymour tells us about the movie he took Aunt Pearl to see. "It said 'adults only,' but I figured how bad could it be? It turned out it was a stag film, Pearl was the only woman there. The things we saw, it was terrible. You wouldn't believe it. I don't know how they let these things go on. . . . I wonder if they're going to have more like it coming."

"Seymour," Grandma says. "Don't give the boy ideas."

"He's still a minor," Grandpa says.

I protest that I am twenty-three.

"That's nothing," Grandpa tells me. "Compared to *us,* you're a minor."

Things weren't always so free, Uncle Seymour informs us. Back in the fifties, when he worked for the studio, there was the Hays Office.

"They had censorship then," Uncle Seymour says. "Today they don't got it. Do you know that they wouldn't let a woman's neckline get too low so too much of her you-know-what showed? I had to cut out those frames from the film.

"Once at a premiere, I met this big actress . . . Very famous star, I can't remember her name now . . . But I says to her after we're introduced, I says, 'I cut you in little pieces.' She looks at me funny, like she doesn't know what I mean. Then I explain: in one scene, a big musical number, I had to cut out frames with her dress too low. She laughed. Then some producer took her away. A very big star at the time . . . I just can't remember her name."

Uncle Seymour is explaining to us how the brain goes when you get old.

"The brain is the size of my fist," he says, demonstrating. "For every fact you remember, there's a fold in the brain. That's why it's got all those wrinkles."

"I eat brains," Grandpa says to me proudly. "You should too. It will make you even smarter." I make a face.

"It's a pity when you get old and can't remember," Uncle

Seymour says. "I was at a wedding two months ago, my brother's granddaughter, and we run into Sadie Kornfeld; you know, the druggist's wife? My brother whispers to me, 'What's her name?' I say, 'What? Are you kidding?' But he says, 'No, for the second I just forgot. I know I know it, but I can't remember.' That's the pity of getting old."

"Yesterday," Grandpa tells us, "I went to the bedroom and by the time I got there, I forgot what I had gone in there for. My mind was a blank. Then, later, I remembered what it was. I needed a handkerchief."

Grandma tells us about Uncle Jerry, who goes around Fort Lauderdale with a note pad and pencil, so he won't forget.

"He writes down everything," Grandma says. "You ask him something and he looks it up on his pad. I tell you, with that pad he's terrific."

Grandma is bothered by her herpes. She can't put on lipstick. She hopes it clears up for Scotty's wedding in two days. We make arrangements for me to take her and Grandpa to the wedding. It is on Long Island, and Grandpa would get lost if he drove himself.

Yesterday Grandma talked to Lynne. Lynne is her daughter-in-law, my aunt by marriage.

"Lynne told me about seeing her Aunt Dora. She went to the hospital and she couldn't believe it was her aunt in the room . . . . The woman looked so different, Lynne had to go right out of the room. Imagine that—Dora was always such a lively person. She went on trips to every state. Even Alaska. She's younger than me."

Grandpa gets angry. "What are you talking about? Dora's in a coma, she don't know anything."

"That's true," Grandma says. "Lynne tells me she's a vegetable."

Grandpa remembers that he hasn't had lunch and he's hungry. He and Grandma go back to their apartment. Uncle Seymour and I are alone on the boardwalk, sitting on one of the few benches left. Stormclouds are moving in from the east.

"You know," Uncle Seymour confides in me, "I don't think you're so innocent. . . . I think it was your bar mitzvah, I think it was you, I came up to you at the end of the affair and I said, 'So, now you're thirteen, you're a man. It's all right now for you to know about everything, about sex. Anything you want to know, just ask me.'

"And you said . . . I think it was you, 'Uncle Seymour, I think I could give *you* some information, not the other way around.' "

He laughs to himself.

It wasn't me, I tell him. At the end of my bar mitzvah, he was in no condition to tell me anything. He was very drunk. They had to carry him out. He and Aunt Pearl didn't speak to each other for weeks.

"Now I just drink one glass a day," he says. "It's good for the heart, the doctor tells me. I even heard a doctor say it on Dinah Shore."

Uncle Seymour puts on his hat. He stretches. "It's time for my constitutional," he says. "I think I'll go over to visit Ike. He's been really bad lately. When you got cancer, nothing goes right. But he's got those cats to keep him company. Your grandma won't go there anymore, the cats are so filthy to her. But a man's got to have something. You know Ike made one of the cats neurotic? They had to have an animal psychiatrist make a house call. I'm not kidding."

I nod.

"And two others have to have operations. With Ike so sick and with no money, he can afford to give cats operations?" Uncle Seymour sighs. "Oh well . . . at least an operation can save *somebody.*"

Uncle Seymour gets up slowly. He has a pacemaker.

I tell him to give Uncle Ike my regards.

"You want to walk over with me?" he asks.

No, I tell him. I just want to sit for awhile.

I watch Uncle Seymour as he walks away, disappearing down the boardwalk. I look behind me, up at Grandma's building. Their terrace door is open; they are having lunch. No doubt they are arguing about something.

It is getting very cloudy. It will start to rain soon.

I stretch out across the bench. Looking down, I spot one of Grandpa's slippers.

Under the boardwalk, some teenagers are drinking beer.

Notes Toward a Story for Uncle Irving

I HAVE TO WRITE a story for Uncle Irving.

I guess I really don't *have* to, but I told him I would, and I suppose I should try.

I told Uncle Irving after he gave me the pen and pencil set: "Now I'll write a story for you."

The gift was a strange gesture.

I had gone to my grandparents' one Sunday afternoon. It was late May and I had just come from the beach. When I reached the door of my grandparents' apartment, I could hear voices inside, not just the usual droning of Grandpa's TV set. It was Uncle Irving and Aunt Birdie. Aunt Birdie is one of Grandpa's sisters. She and Uncle Irving live in the next building from my grandparents'. When I see them on the street or on the boardwalk, I usually try to avoid them. As a general rule they make me nervous.

But Uncle Irving going all the way back to his apartment in the other building just to get me the pen and pencil set—it was really quite strange. Grandma said it was because I said "Hello, Uncle Irving" to him when I came in and I was smiling when I said it, like I was glad to see him. "It was calling him by name like that that did it," Grandma said. "He doesn't get too much respect. It was like an honor for him." An honor to be called *Uncle Irving?* I guess it was. For a few minutes later, he jumped up and said, "I have to get something for Richard." Just like that. It was all very peculiar. Even Aunt Birdie looked at him strangely; she hasn't liked me in years, I think—not that I care. But I never thought Uncle Irving liked me either, although I hadn't given the matter much thought. Yet I suppose I tolerate him as much as anyone will. Uncle Irving is nuts.

"No, no," everyone said, "don't bother, not now," but Uncle Irving was adamant. In ten minutes he was back with a pen and pencil set for me. He said he had gotten several of them from his brother Ruby, the bank president. Uncle Irving wanted me to have one. I was actually touched.

"I figured you got more call to use it than me, you being a writer and all." He was grinning. "I'm not a writer. I don't get much call to use them."

"Thank you, Uncle Irving," I told him. "This is really nice." There was a ball-point pen and a cartridge pen with two ink cartridges and a mechanical pencil with an eraser under its cap. "Now I'll write a story for you," I said.

"Yeah, sure," he said, kind of sarcastically. But he was really happy that I'd said that; you could tell. And even though I know he's a nut it still made me feel good to make him happy. After all, it really wasn't much trouble. So I said again, "No, I really mean it, I'm going to write a story for you, Uncle Irving."

And that's how it started. That's why a story is necessary.

I never told Uncle Irving, but I had a lot of trouble with the cartridge pen. In putting in the cartridge I must have done something wrong (I'm not very mechanical) and I ended up splattering blue ink all over the place. Mostly on my pants. Luckily I was only wearing a pair of old dungarees. But I decided that was enough for the cartridges. The ball-point was okay, but what I really prefer is a Bic Accountant Fine Point.

My handwriting is pretty small, and I need very thin lines to squeeze everything I write into my diary each night. Keeping a diary is very important for a writer, I haven't missed a day since the day I started writing, on August 8, 1969. Writing every day gives you discipline. It's also good to get your thoughts down permanently, because things like that tend to get away otherwise. And it's good for the future, when people do their master's theses on you and stuff. So I didn't use the ball-point very much. The pencil was okay, but I don't have much use for a pencil. I don't do artwork or math or crossword puzzles, just writing. The eraser part comes in handy, though, for when I'm typing up a story and I have to correct a mistake. I only use erasable typing paper. I can't get that Ko-Rec-Type to work properly and besides, it supposedly gets into your machine. And Liquid Paper's too messy and spillable.

I guess, knowing Uncle Irving, he'd like the story to be about himself. He's kind of self-centered, I suppose; actually, I think he's paranoid and maybe worse, the way he messed up his only kid like that. But who am I to make diagnoses? I'm a writer, not a shrink; I have no right.

Uncle Irving, Uncle Irving, what do I know about you?

1. You and Aunt Birdie used to have a nut store on Caton Avenue, which is kind of funny, you both being nuts and all, but there's not much of a story in that beyond the one joke.

2. You and Aunt Birdie have a pretty crazy way of living now that you're retired. I guess it comes from you working nights for so long. You get up around 4:00 A.M. (sometimes I don't even get to bed by then; but after all, I'm young and a writer and I have girlfriends and insomnia), you eat breakfast, you watch TV, you have lunch at about ten-thirty in the morning, maybe you go shopping or visit or go for a walk, you

have dinner at about 3:00 P.M., and are in bed usually around 8:00 P.M. It's a strange way to live; that might make an interesting story, about a couple who lives like that.

3. You're bald. Once you thought you'd make a lot of money by finding a cure for baldness. Your mother-in-law, my great-grandmother, told you she had a remedy from the old country and you tried it on yourself first, to see how it would work. The method involved pumpkin and rum. First you baked pumpkin, the insides of it, in the oven and then you mixed rum in with it and put the stuff all over your bald head, holding it there with a towel wrapped around like a turban. You stayed home from work for a week and kept it on all the time, day and night. Finally, around the fifth day, it began to stink like anything. Aunt Birdie yelled at you: "Irving! Take it off! It's fermenting!" And you did and there still wasn't a hair on your head and your money-making dreams were wrecked again and you smelled terrible besides. Readers might find that amusing in a story, especially if I say that your mother-in-law made the whole thing up just to see what a jerk you were.

4. One thing that really isn't funny at all is that you're paranoid. You didn't speak to Aunt Birdie for three weeks recently just because another man asked her to dance with him at the senior citizens' center. Even when I was a little kid, I remember, I'd see you at the beach telling men not to look at Aunt Birdie the wrong way. You would yell at senile old men, middle-aged men, teenage boys even. Did you really think a guy in his twenties would find Aunt Birdie attractive? She must have been fifty then, and pretty plump, and with those buck teeth, she surely wasn't the most attractive thing on two legs. And you're really a bitter man, because you never "made it." You say you never "made it" because of all the people who were jealous of you and were out to get you, like those Irish secretaries at Twentieth Century Fox. When you worked there

I used to think you were something big at the studio because you got me all those movie posters and the things from that Arabian movie, but I was a kid then and not very aware of things. Now I know you were only the night watchman. I don't think those two Irish secretaries could've hurt you with the big boss if they tried. They probably didn't even notice you. Like with blacks—you think every black man you pass on the street has it on his mind to rape Aunt Birdie. And you tell me that blacks don't have to pay fares on buses anymore; the other day you said, "Now they have the upper hand, that's for sure." And all your big schemes went nowhere; you complain that you're everybody's poor relation, but my grandparents don't have any more money than you, and they don't complain all the time. I know, I know—it was always the other guy who got rich, the guy who stole your ideas. Those Jolly Jumpers, that nut store, the Bellechase mining stock the whole family lost money on—everything you do ended badly, *not* because the other guy cheated you, "the big wheels of the world who are only out for themselves." No, it was because of *you,* Uncle Irving.

5. Other miscellaneous things: You're afraid to step out on Grandma's terrace. We laugh at you when you're not around. You tell the same stories over and over again, like how those Gentile kids used to beat you up in Brownsville. You tell me that I break out because at my age I'm "hot-blooded" and that when I marry, my acne will clear up; yet you're seventy-five and you still get pimples. You once confessed to me that you went to a whorehouse in the old days and I spent hours vainly trying to imagine you there. You have a wife who's afraid to go to the dentist, afraid that she'll gag, afraid that somehow someone's going to slip something unkosher into her food and she'll get sick because of it. You got dead drunk at my bar mitzvah and they had to carry you out; Aunt Birdie didn't talk to you for a long time after that, and yet at Cousin Chick's

wedding you did the same thing all over again, throwing up right on the dance floor. You don't know anything about politics and yet you talk like you're the big expert on it. When you were fired from your last job, you ended up selling gloves on a street corner. You have contributed absolutely nothing to society and you ruined Teddy's life.

Yes—Teddy. You never talk about him, but I know some things, from my grandparents, even though I've never seen Teddy. That he was in all those institutions and nothing helped him. That you used to drive him crazy, following him around everywhere to see that he didn't get dirty from other kids, making him wear sweaters in ninety-degree heat, telling him one thing and then the other till finally he went crazy just to get away from you and Aunt Birdie. So now he's out and he's a grown man and he's been involved with drugs and he was a pimp and he carried a cane with a sword inside it to protect himself from his enemies. Now he lives in some slum and calls himself a minister of a new religion and has a plan to save all the sinners in this city. Like my grandfather, your brother-in-law, says, "It's a pity on Teddy." And it's a shame on you, Uncle Irving, you ignorant, boastful, cowardly, neurotic, foolish old man.

Driving Slow

WE ARE IN A CADILLAC. There are five of us. We are driving back from the cemetery after burying my uncle. We are driving slow.

My father is the driver. He is smoking a Pall Mall cigarette although the man we just buried, his brother-in-law, had died of lung cancer. "You better stop," Uncle Leon told my father. But my father is nervous and has business worries so bad that his vision is sometimes blocked by a herringbone pattern. In the morning it hurts to hear him cough. He is half a century old. Not one of his hairs is grey. His lungs are grey though.

Next to him sits his father, my grandfather. My grandfather is staring out the car window. He reads all of the signs aloud as we drive on the Southern State Parkway. He is wearing sunglasses and smoking a cigar. My grandfather is half again as old as my father. My father is twice my age. My grandfather has lived exactly three times as long as I have. It is such a neat progression: 25, 50, 75. You wonder where it will end.

In the back seat there are three of us. I am surrounded by two women. It seems I am always in the middle. When I was younger and we went on school trips I would say that I had to have the window seat on the bus because I got carsick.

On my left is my grandmother. She is weeping. No one has

suffered the way she has, she will be the first to tell you that. This latest blow, her daughter's husband's death, has been perhaps the last straw. She has been a semi-invalid for years and is always on the verge of dying. She had me worried at the cemetery. She put my hand on her breast. Her heart was beating wildly. My grandmother whispered, almost triumphantly, "That's angina," and she placed a nitroglycerin tablet under her tongue. Now she weeps into a yellow lace handkerchief. She says nothing except for a few words: "That old witch." She is talking about my uncle's mother, another bitter woman.

My cousin Patty is sitting on the other side of me. The night before when I called her to tell her Leon was dead she said, "My mother has no luck with husbands." By this she means that her own father had died when she was just sixteen and now her stepfather is dead as well. They were buried not far apart, actually, each in his own family plot. After the services my aunt and her first husband's sister wanted to know if they could visit Patty's father's grave but my father said it wasn't right, that it would take away from burying Uncle Leon. To me my father said: "How much can your aunt take?"

My cousin Patty has been married once. She has had a son. She has had an abortion. She has lived alone and with a black drug addict and with an Israeli psychologist and with another divorced woman. Her ex-husband is watching their baby. Her ex-in-laws came to the funeral. My father said it was a nice gesture but my grandmother said it didn't cost them anything.

At the end Uncle Leon spoke like Donald Duck. This was because of the radiation treatments.

At the end Uncle Leon looked like his own father. I had never seen his father, but this is whom I imagined him to look like.

At the end he couldn't swallow food. At the end it was a heart attack or pneumonia. "It's always a heart attack or pneumonia," my grandfather says. But when he dies next year, it will be a stroke.

We are driving slow because we are following a car and because there is a car following us.

In front of us is a Pacer containing Patty's brother, my cousin, who is driving and who is younger than me; his wife of two weeks, who is also younger than me; my aunt, the widow for the second time, who is older than my father; and my aunt's first husband's sister, who took me aside at the cemetery to tell me she had a husband, three brothers and a sister buried not far away.

I can only see the back of four heads. I can only wonder what they are saying, or if they are saying anything.

In back of us is a Chevrolet. My younger brother is driving. This has been the first time he has ever gone to a funeral. He was too young or too frightened the other times. He had to smoke marijuana this morning before he could go. Next to him sits my mother. She is chewing sugarless gum. When I turn my head she almost looks like Farrah Fawcett-Majors. She has almost the same nose, almost the same hair. My mother is one of those beautiful women who have never thought about death.

Behind my mother, in the back seat of the Chevy, sit her mother and father, my other grandparents. They try not to think about death, either. They are in their late sixties.

We are a wagon train, I think, a wagon train traveling west along the Southern State Parkway of Long Island, and I imagine that we are rolling along the Oregon Trail. As I am imagining this, my father, unable to stand the silence and his mother's weeping, turns on the car's stereo. We hear someone sing—"Help me, I'm falling in love . . ." and my grandfather says, “Shut that damn thing off.” My father does so. My grandmother continues to weep. My grandfather continues to read signs, “Exit 35, Peninsula Boulevard North.” My cousin Patty continues to look in her pocketbook for some valium. My father continues to drive. Behind us my brother drives. In front of us my cousin drives. We yawn from exhaustion and our stomachs growl with hunger. At my aunt’s house there is food waiting for us, food prepared by her son’s mother-in-law. There are hard-boiled eggs and Danish pastries and cold cuts and salad. My mother’s father is especially hungry; he has diabetes.

It starts to rain. Soon it *is* raining. It is going to rain for a while. Yesterday it rained for a few hours. The day before it had rained for the whole day. Tomorrow it will probably rain too, and maybe the day after that as well.

We are thirteen people in three cars and we are all going to die. One grandfather will die very soon. The other will die in ten years. My grandmother will weep for another twenty years, surprising us all. My father will continue to smoke Pall Malls. My mother will stay beautiful. My cousins will be divorced. Patty will marry again. My aunt will one day move to another state, where she will live alone but happily. Her former sister-in-law will make us all laugh back at the house. My brother will smoke marijuana in the bathroom. My other grandmother will have a dizzy spell. And we will all read magazines and have surgery and wish for more money than we ever seem to have at the moment. And one day, a long time from now, I will meet someone I saw at today’s funeral and she will be so thrilled to see me and she will get up and hug me and then start to cry. I will say, “What’s wrong?” and she will tell me: “Oh, Richard, I’m so *old!*” And then I will realize I am older than she is.

Meanwhile we drive slow.

WOMEN

The Princess from the Land of Porcelain

HER MOTHER DIED in May of 1962, the day after Memorial Day, the day Adolf Eichmann was hanged. She was thirteen at the time. She spent the summer with the family of her aunt, her father's sister. It was at a bungalow colony in the Catskills.

Every few weeks Leslie would go with her aunt's family to see summer stock at the theatre in Forestburg. The theatre was in an old converted barn. After the show, instead of taking curtain calls, the actors, in costume, would form a receiving line in the lobby. They would shake hands with the exiting audience. Leslie would take care to shake each actor's hand. Then, once outside in the cricket-chirping night, she would lick her entire hand with her tongue. Mostly she tasted sweat.

She was thirteen and a half when she menstruated. After three months, her periods stopped. Another seven months and she told her aunt, who took her to the doctor. The doctor prescribed tranquilizers. Leslie took two and had her period again the next day. After that, she was fairly regular.

She majored in Russian in college and went to law school. Then she got a job with the SEC in Washington. She married a very rich boy whose father owned a chain of men's clothing stores on Long Island. What she liked about Evan was that he was *pliable.* And he looked like Mark Spitz. They lived apart: he in New York, she in Washington. They met on weekends. It was an open marriage. Evan made Leslie happy. Her favorite novel was *The Eternal Husband.* When she got to be an old lady she would make a new translation of it.

Her specialty was Chapter Eleven, the section of the Federal Bankruptcy Law dealing with corporations. But at the SEC they had her investigating mutual funds frauds. It was a dreary business. She developed a nervous stomach, starting relying on Titrilac more. She took a yoga course, but it didn't go well. "You must loosen up more," the instructor would tell her.

"I'm sorry, Miss Shastri," she would say. "But this is as loose as I come."

Her father was a linguistics professor at the University of Minnesota. He still looked good when she saw him, which wasn't often. Neither of them were letter-writers.

Ken was her lover. Mostly he was gay. But it was a calm, low-key affair: what she needed. Evan was seeing his old girlfriend in New York during the week. She needed someone too. Ken was available. He managed a movie theatre on Connecticut Avenue. He didn't ever cry the way Evan did. Ken was even an acquaintance of Evan's girl Sari. It was that kind of a small world.

When she first asked Ken what he did, he told her he twisted slowly, slowly in the wind. She laughed. They had casual sex, nothing very heavy. Ken used to come to her apartment and stare at the photograph she had of Evan. He also thought Evan looked like Mark Spitz.

She once told Ken he didn't seem particularly gay. When she asked him why he didn't call himself bisexual, he told her she wouldn't be able to understand. And about being particularly gay: "Oh, I'm particular. And I'm gay, too."

When Ken's theatre had a Frank Capra revival, Leslie cried at the end of "It's a Wonderful Life." She felt embarrassed afterwards.

Every night at eleven, Evan would call her. He seemed to approve of Ken. Or of what Leslie told him about Ken. Evan himself was too involved with Sari to intrude on Leslie's business. There were private things that did not require any discussions between them. Leslie and her husband operated on trust. They both had lots of psychic space. Everyone did. Ken had his Senate page, apart from Leslie. Sari was living with a radical therapist who rather liked Evan. It was all in the open.

Leslie and Ken both called in sick one day and went to see the Peacock Room in the Freer Gallery: enormous, lusciously feathered peacocks on the shuttered windows; turquoise-painted leather ceilings; the portrait of the Princess from the Land of Porcelain—*Harmony in Blue and Gold.* The painting showed a young woman in a creamy kimono standing in front of a pastel sixfold screen. It was elegant, somewhat Oriental, somehow very comforting. While they were sitting on the bench, Ken told her he was leaving Washington. She was surprised at how surprised she was.

Ken put down his cup of herb tea and looked at her.

"Are you throwing a silent temper tantrum because I'm going away?"

She made herself look innocent. "Who, me?" she said. And some of the tension melted.

She kissed his cheek. She quoted Gogol. *"Skúchno na étom svéte, gospodà."*

"And what does that mean?"

She blew her nose. " 'It's gloomy in this world, gentlemen.' "

"Don't overdramatize."

That night she didn't sleep. She had a cold. The post-nasal drip was keeping her awake. She had nightmares too, even though she wasn't quite asleep. In the morning she called in sick and it was true.

She wanted to be taken care of. That was the part that made her feel so guilty.

She called Evan in New York. She hinted around, hoping he would say "poor baby" and take the next shuttle to Washington. But he didn't, of course. He made a joke, told her it was *appalling* that a person like her should get a cold. She didn't get it.

"You take all that Vitamin C," his voice over the phone said. "Like Linus Pauling says. A-Pauling, get it?"

She hung up the phone.

He called back and said, "I love you."

"I love you too."

He was having a problem with the Huntington store, he said. He couldn't talk to her too long. She told him that was all right.

She went to the Lincoln Memorial at night, despite the cold. She wanted to see if it was true what Ken had told her, that Lincoln's statue smiled from one side and frowned from the other side. She was impressed, enough to tell some stranger about it, a hip-looking guy from Colorado.

"Schizophrenia, that's all," the Colorado guy said. "Why not?

After all, it's the American national disease." He gave her what she knew was supposed to be a meaningful look. "How schizophrenic are you?" he asked her.

She smiled, took the Fifth Amendment, and moved on.

She reached for a Contac and wondered if the Age of Anxiety had given way to the Age of Possibilities. No more "shoulds." Growth was the king. Everyone was growing—not up or down or tall or fat—just growing. Living like Topsy they all were.

Her nightgown was worn so thin it was nearly transparent. She had some Darvon in her medicine cabinet and she debated whether to take one. Wooziness might help. Her arms and legs ached, like the "growing pains" she felt as a girl. In the end she decided against the Darvon. It might not mix with the cold capsule she was taking.

She wondered if she should do something. But she didn't know what she had anything to do *about.* She was separated from Evan by an hour's flight, Ken hadn't left town yet—so why did it matter, being alone? Questions formed in her head. Iffy questions, the kind General Eisenhower used to talk about. Then she realized that she wasn't satisfied with her life.

She thought of her operation at New York Eye and Ear when she was only five. The muscles of her right eye had been weak, and the eye was turning inward. Her mother slept in the hospital room with her, both the night before surgery and for two days afterward. When Leslie got out of the hospital she had to wear a special pair of glasses with one red-colored lens. She was in first grade, standing outside the school at 8:30 on a cold morning when a fat Chinese boy came over to her and said:

"Hey, Red Eye! You should be on television!"

She didn't say anything to the boy then. Now she wished she had killed him.

When Evan first brought up the possibility of marriage, she told him she didn't know if she loved him.

"If you think you're in love, then that's love, Les," he had said. " 'I think I love you' is as good as 'I love you.' "

At the time she thought she loved him. She still supposed he was right. But maybe she was just incapable of love.

She watched a made-for-television movie in which a with-it heroine ran away to find herself. But Leslie didn't have to find herself and she didn't believe in running away. Of course she could always start therapy again. But she lacked the energy for that.

She could not sleep. Her cold had become worse. She couldn't stifle her cough, nor keep her throat from getting dry, nor stop her head from hurting.

She drank some pineapple juice, went back to bed, got up again. Leslie remembered an article that said you could cure insomnia if you kept your tongue tucked into your cheek for a long period of time. She tried it while sitting in her kitchenette. She felt foolish so she put her tongue back where it belonged.

She tried to read what she thought was an irresponsible book: *How to Prepare for the Next Great Depression.* Another woman lawyer at the SEC had given it to her.

Leslie got annoyed with the author after thirty pages. Granted, things did not look good; still, one shouldn't panic people. She put the book away.

It was 3:17. Evan had made her a digital clock. He was so clever at things like that, but he still felt he was better off working for his father.

It was 3:18. She wanted so desperately to sleep. She started to cry. Leslie cried for several minutes, then went to the bathroom mirror to look at herself. Her eyes were red. She tried smiling broadly, just to see herself smiling with swollen red eyes. Her throat hurt when she swallowed.

She thought of a sign she and Evan saw on their cross-country trip. *Drive Carefully,* the sign said, *We Love Our Children.*

Since college Leslie had been waiting for someone to call her *Duska*: "little soul" in Russian. She knew that Evan would call her that if she asked him to, but that would have meant asking him to, and there was no point in that.

Evan's clock said it was 3:43.

Before she finally slept, she said "I love you" aloud. She didn't have the slightest idea whom she was talking to.

She was walking along the campus of the University of Pennsylvania, where she had gone to law school. Clouds were overhead, threatening. Suddenly she started running, past the library, running quickly. She was off campus, running up the Franklin Parkway, passing the hilltop hulk of the art museum alongside the Schuylkill.

Leslie was not surprised at how fast she was running. She reached her aunt's bungalow colony in the Catskills in no time. It was still raining and it was becoming night. She opened the door of the bungalow.

Sari, Evan's Sari, was inside, sitting on a waterbed by the floor. She was wearing a kimono with a red sash, just like the girl in Whistler's painting, the one Ken had taken her to see.

"I lost my pocketbook running," Leslie whined.

Sari remained serene. "That's all right."

Leslie wondered if Evan was around; but she was afraid to ask Sari.

"If I were you," Sari said, getting up from the waterbed, "I would have done things differently."

"But if I were you, I would have done *your* things differently," Leslie protested.

Sari just smiled. She loosened her sash and undid the top half of her kimono, slipping it around her waist. Her breasts were bare. They were full and pendulous, unlike Leslie's, and her nipples were within Leslie's reach.

"It's still raining," Sari said softly.

Leslie listened for the rain on the roof. From the window came a moment of lightning. No thunder followed it. Leslie felt secure. She was safely inside, safe with Sari. Sari seemed so sure of herself.

She felt what she knew was love. She touched Sari's breast with one finger. Then another. With her fingers she drew circles around Sari's nipples. She bent over to kiss them.

She stirred out of sleep. She tried to get back into the dream.

Aspects of Ann

In her senior year in high school she played Portia in *Julius Caesar.* It was a small part but she was one of only two women in the play. She went on one night when she had very bad cramps. People told her she was good. She liked being Portia, especially the speech when Portia tells Brutus that she is a woman well-reputed, stronger than her sex:

> I have made strong proof of my constancy,
> Giving myself a voluntary wound
> Here, in the thigh: can I bear that with patience,
> And not my husband's secrets?

The director wanted her to show the wound on her thigh. Ann felt it wasn't necessary and refused to do it. Later the director told her that she had probably been right.

When people asked her if she was an only child, Ann usually said yes. If they were people whom she felt she could really come to know, she told them about her retarded younger brother.

"Why do you dress like a dyke?" a new friend once asked her in the middle of a conversation about the Cumaean Sibyl.

Ann thought of her turtleneck sweaters and jeans and Pro-Keds and said, "I *like* to look dykey." She knew that would set the new friend wondering, and she was glad.

Paul was her first husband, a classicist, a capital-R romantic. She had slept with so many boys during the first year of college and she hated sex. Then Paul came along, very thin and very smart and very good looking. After that sex was something she never wanted to stop doing. They got married in their senior year at Bucknell.

Other guys made passes at Paul and he went through a period of thinking he was gay. Ann, unfazed, told him, "Why don't you do it instead of just thinking about it?" And then she got pregnant.

It was before 1970 and the illegal abortionist came to their apartment from Jersey City and Ann passed out while it was being done on the kitchen table. A month later the doctor in the next apartment from Ann's and Paul's was arrested for performing abortions. Both of them doted on the irony.

In Hamburg she met a boy named Joachim who had of course blond hair and muscles. He was a swimmer and had just missed going to the '68 Olympics in Mexico City. They slept together and he joked that because of their names he shouldn't use a condom. Ann just wondered about that but the thought crept out during the night. Joachim spoke excellent English and could make puns.

Years later she read that Joachim was the name of Anne's husband in the New Testament. Together Joachim and Anne were the parents of the Blessed Virgin Mary.

Then came The Movement and living with a bunch of people in the East Village. Those were the nostalgia days. She got pregnant again, from a man in the house named Marty. The first person she told about it was her ex-husband Paul.

"You're going to have it, aren't you?" Paul said.

"Yes, I think so."

"Why now and not then?"

"I don't know."

"You must."

"No, really."

In her fifth month she gave in to parental hysteria and married Marty with her fingers crossed. Three months after Jasmine was born Ann had another affair, another series of scenes, a second divorce.

"I don't want to fall in love again," she told her mother.

"Nonsense," her mother said. "One day it'll happen and you'll be happy like everyone else."

Ann decided it was wiser not to respond to that.

Nights she spent with the *Oxford English Dictionary.*

When Jasmine was in kindergarten she came home one day and said she was going to get married.

"To who?" said Ann, reading an Indian folklore book.

"I don't know yet," Jasmine told her. "To a boy."

"Why not to a girl?"

Jasmine snorted condescendingly. "Girls can't marry *girls.* Our teacher said so."

"Well," said Ann the mother, "your teacher doesn't know everything."

At thirty-five her ex-husband Marty asked his mother for $10,000 in reparations. He wanted the money as compensation for her years of screwing him up. When Ann took Jasmine to see her grandmother, Marty's mother, the woman asked Ann, "Do you think he's nuts?"

Ann thought for a moment over her Constant Comment tea. "Yeah," she told her former mother-in-law. "I do."

Paul and his friend would sometimes visit Ann and Jasmine, and Ann was glad that Paul was close to another man. She didn't know if they were sleeping together, and she didn't ask, but she could see that there was something close between them and that was what Paul needed.

She never overheard Paul's friend tell him, "The most amazing thing about Ann is the way she smiles. Not just with her mouth but with her whole face."

There was a beautiful woman in the next office at the museum and Ann was a little in love with her. One day Ann was waiting for the elevator and she saw someone go over to this beautiful woman and call her Mrs. Farrell, which was Ann's name. The someone blushed and saw Ann and said, "I'm sorry, but the two of you look so much alike."

That made Ann's day that day.

When her distribution map of grooved stone axes in Pennsylvania was finished, the curator told her that she had made "a real contribution." He smiled eerily as he said it. But Ann knew that she was the first to realize a pattern of distribution.

"Jasmine dropped a chopstick down the drain last night," she wrote Paul, "and I waded through quarts of larded water until the sink finally unclogged itself this afternoon. I've intended to learn something about plumbing for years—this may have provided the impetus I needed."

Two days after her brother choked to death during lunch at the institution, the pathologist told her that there was no malignancy. Ann did not feel ecstatically happy.

If it had been cancer, she would have thought: "Why me?"

Instead she thought: "Why *not* me?"

That night, after putting Jasmine to bed, she stared a long while at her own thigh.

Kirchbachstrasse 121, 2800 Bremen

NOTHING MUCH IS HAPPENING.

Helmut and Mara build boxes for the stereo speakers.

Tomorrow they will go to the park.

Easter. Helmut's mother comes in with one egg. It is a brandy egg. She leaves it on the table. Helmut and Mara are out.

Mara takes the brats to a carnival. She puts them on rides, they eat all sorts of crap, and they play those hit-the-ball-and-win-a-prize games. Mara thinks: This is *weird.* She is hassled by the kids screaming for money and wanting to go on this ride and that one. Then they have to take a streetcar and a bus back to the kids' house and put them in bed for their mother. Mara passes a mirror and makes an ugly face. The face looks back at her.

Helmut says his feet are cold in bed.

"If you don't think about it," Mara tells him, "you won't get depressed."

Helmut says he is having a hard time adjusting.

Someone offers Helmut and Mara 150 American dollars to translate an article for a conference at the University. They try their best to do it. Helmut translates and Mara corrects his English and then types out the article. After that, they make love again. Helmut's feet are still cold.

Helmut and Mara go to a farm for the weekend. It is forty minutes from Bremen, out in the country. Twelve of Helmut's friends live on the farm's commune. Mara is disgusted by the mice. But the surrounding fields are beautiful. Four members of the commune are a rock band. Helmut says their music is far-out when they rehearse.

At the farmhouse, Mara has bad dreams. She suspects they are indicative of something. In one dream she eats part of her diaphragm. Helmut thinks Mara's dreams are fun to remember and talk about at the pub. Helmut never dreams. Mara sometimes wishes he were unhappy more of the time, but she is afraid of them both being unhappy at the same time.

The stereo is not working again. Helmut says he will fix it when he has time. Right now he is so busy. Mara gets into one of her bad moods again. They never fight. He asks her if she is homesick. She says nothing, just kisses his knee.

Mara thinks: Helmut does things so slowly. I have come to have no expectations at this point. I am much too young for that. But there is no place else I want to be.

For a moment, drying his wet blond hair, Helmut looks nothing short of beautiful.

Mara goes to the mailbox. No letter from Nick yet. She is quite blue by now; she will write to him, waiting for him to answer her letter. Helmut thinks Nick is no good. Other friends from America confirm this judgment.

Mara is unemployed again and running out of money at an alarming rate. She is going to try to get her resident permit at last. She is not making much progress. There are so many forms. Helmut's attitude is *mañana, mañana,* but he is prepared to lend her money if she needs it. But Mara is too proud and too angry to borrow any money. She will ask her friend Rose what to do.

All of Europe is under a strange and unforseen temperature

turnabout, Mara reads in the *International Herald Tribune.* Fruit trees are blooming in January. It is unseasonably warm. The newspaper cannot explain why.

"It is a terrible newspaper," Mara writes Nick. "You can't even understand some articles because of typographical errors."

It is strange and beautiful for awhile, in the nook of dawn. Mara always wakes before Helmut. Before Mara came, he needed three alarm clocks and a mother. While Helmut is dressing, Mara prepares breakfast. She has to be careful not to use too much water when she boils an egg. She thinks of the one brandy egg Helmut's mother brought for Easter.

"I think I'll stay with Helmut until it's time for me to go," Mara writes Nick. She is not even sure he still lives in Boston. "There are many problems," she writes. "Mostly money and furniture."

But she smiles as she looks out the window.

The divorced businesswoman tells Mara she need not look after the brats anymore. Mara needs the money, but the children's aunt is coming from Greece for the rest of the year. The aunt is their great-aunt, a Greek woman, their father's aunt. The father disappeared long ago.

The divorced businesswoman sees the look on Mara's face. So she says she can help her. Mara can sell ice cream in one of her stores. It is in the suburbs, in the shopping center, only an hour away.

Mara says she will do it.

Helmut has a new job. He is a sound mixer for his friends' rock band. He sits in front of a huge sound machine and pushes a lot of buttons. While he does it he smokes. He has to go to all the rehearsals, and that means two nights a week. But

Mara does not say anything. She is told that she has begun to bite her nails.

Helmut and Mara pretend they are on vacation. They do not have enough money to go away, so they take a trip in fantasy. Helmut gets into a bad accident on the Yugoslavian highway, and Mara is killed. She is buried with all the others, by the side of the road. Helmut wanted to take her body to Greece, but the Yugoslav authorities would not permit that. So he goes on to Greece alone, feeling guilty but rather relieved. He gets a case of dysentery and a bad sunburn. He runs out of money in Athens. In a Japanese restaurant there are bugs in his food. He returns to the side of the Yugoslavian highway and curls up beside Mara's grave. He hears her snickering.

In reality, there is no trip, of course. They are still in bed, making love. It is Sunday morning. Helmut is always so cold.

It has been nine months since Nick has written. Mara thinks: A baby could have been born by now.

There is no marijuana in Bremen. Only hash. Mara and Helmut get very stoned twice a week, on Wednesdays and Saturdays. They always have a hilariously nice time. Helmut and Mara type each other love letters on his typewriter. They take turns. Helmut hasn't the slightest idea of how the typewriter works, so his love letters are better. They make Mara laugh and laugh.

It is the crux of the matter, she thinks silently. Or the meat of the flesh or something like that. I am maliciously stoned. Who needs Nick?

Mara gets sick on the charcoal-grilled bratwursts. She feels so out of touch with Germany. This is no country she lives in. It is all Helmut's world. Helmutland, she thinks, as once again the vomit rises up in huge waves and engulfs her.

Helmut and Mara unwind in the evening. They bathe together. They decide to go downtown and drink a beer or six in the various pubs. They meet a few people, including a half-Cherokee, half-Jewish American who takes to Mara right away. His name is Mark. He lives with a Belgian woman by whom he has had a child. The child, a girl, was born in Brussels. Mark and the child's mother named her after Mark's mother: Lahoma. But the Belgian authorities do not permit it; they say Lahoma is not a real name. Mark has to write Oklahoma for proof. Finally his mother's death certificate arrives; it is too many months later. But the Belgian authorities insist on the birth certificate of the mother. They say the death certificate is of no value. Again Mark writes to Oklahoma. The letter gets lost in the mail. Finally, Mark gives up. And takes his woman and still-unnamed child to Bremen.

In the present, Mara listens to the story. It is four in the morning, an hour after dawn. She realizes that she has begun to smoke cigarettes.

Mara wants to go to the North Sea. Helmut has too much work to do. Go alone, he tells her. But she wants to know how he will get up in the morning without her. Helmut sighs and says he can manage. But Mara feels guilty and decides to stay home.

She finally gets a letter from Nick. He is living in Chicago now; he got her address from a friend of her sister's. The letter is in the style Mara knows as inimitably Nick's. Nick is getting more egotistical than ever and that is hard to imagine. Mara tells Helmut she thought it was impossible for Nick to get worse. Nick brags about his friends in the mayor's office. Plus he sends his photograph, from one of those four-for-a-quarter booths. Helmut gets quietly angry. Finally Mara convinces him it is just Nick's way. She lets him rub her back that night.

The ice-cream selling is not going well. The flavors are vanilla, chocolate, banana, strawberry, orange and waldmeister. But they are only powder, water and air. So much air. Like everything else, Mara thinks, it is swelled with mere air.

Rose is finally able to persuade Mara to go to Berlin for a few days. Mara does not enjoy herself. Berlin reminds her of Cambridge. When she returns she finds Helmut and Mark at a party. They are as high as kites, but Helmut is anxious to see her. Mara has been thinking all along coming back on the Autobahn: This must be a very passionate reunion, or it is no good at all.

When Mara wakes up, she decides it was a passionate reunion after all. Maybe not *very* passionate, but passionate enough for her to stay. While Helmut is asleep she gets out Nick's picture, tears it up, and is sorry.

Helmut teases Mara for not being able to keep up with the drinking habits of Germans. Mara nearly always ends up getting sick. They are only having fun, but it turns out to be a real argument.

Still, they have to be quiet now. Mark has left his woman and child and moved in with them. He contributes some money to the household, but not enough. Most of the day he stays home and studies the Torah. His father was Jewish, he tells them, but he ran away before Mark was born. Now he wants to get in touch with his roots.

Helmut suggests they all go to Dachau. Mark is enthusiastic but Mara says they will have to drag her there. Helmut and Mark go to Dachau without her.

Alone, Mara thinks: I hope they both become lampshades. She writes a long letter to Nick in Chicago, ignoring his personality once again.

Helmut's mother gives him some things for Christmas. Helmut and Mara do not have a Christmas tree, a Tannenbaum. Their apartment is too small. Especially with Mark there now. Mara is growing to despise him, despite his being American. She wonders if she will eventually become like Mark. She asks Helmut to throw him out. Helmut says Mark will only be there another week or so. Mara is silently furious. While Helmut is at work she sleeps with Mark. It is no worse than she had imagined.

The next morning Mark leaves and goes back to his woman and child.

Mara's weaving is not working out as she had planned. She needs more practice. Sometimes she gets very depressed and feels like going to Boulder to live with her sister. But that is only at odd moments. She wouldn't know what to do without that part of herself named Helmut. Mara has stopped talking of her problems, because she thinks she has begun to frighten Helmut for the first time.

The landlady lowers the rent because they are so poor. Mara knows that Helmut could charm the pants off the landlady if he wanted to. That is Helmut's gift: he can make people do things they really would like to do but wouldn't without him.

Mara thinks: in German *gift* means poison.

They get stoned and Mara believes she can fly out the window. It is really a bad scene. Helmut tries to convince her that she cannot fly. Mara insists she can. He feels her head; she is feverish. Scared, he puts her to bed. He stays with her all night as she talks deliriously, endlessly, in a stream of three languages at once.

By mid-morning Mara's fever is down.

Helmut notices how pale Mara still is. He wonders aloud if they should perhaps go to Amsterdam during the summer. That would not be too expensive, he tells her. For no reason, Mara begins to cry. She knows she is scaring him, but she cannot help herself. It is too much effort to try.

Helmut slides off Mara's tiny body. She is getting as thin as he. They are both sweaty. He looks toward the wall and finally says it. Mara doesn't say anything. She doesn't even cry. Tears are useless at this point.

In two weeks she buys her airline ticket.

Surprisingly, there is another letter from Nick. Helmut looks at the envelope all morning. But Mara will not open it. She says she will leave it for Helmut. Something to amuse him afterwards.

He wants to go to Amsterdam with her. He wants to see her get on the plane.

No, she says. Please. It is difficult enough. Besides, there are examinations to be taken.

Forty-seven times she wants to tell him to forget the stupid examinations; forty-seven times she does not tell him this. They have stopped making love.

The apartment is empty. Oh, there is furniture there, and most everything. But Mara is gone. She left without saying goodbye. All of her things have disappeared. She left some things with Mark, other things with Rose: whatever she did not take with her. For Helmut, there is no evidence that she ever existed in that place. Nothing but Nick's letter. On the envelope Mara has written: *I miss you so much and I'm still here.*

Helmut sighs, sits down at the kitchen table. He puts on the stereo.

The music is very loud.

Helmut studies his own hand for several seconds. Then he decides to go out. Maybe Mark or the others will want to do something.

Helmut stretches; Mara is in his mind; Helmut goes toward the door; he is not thinking of Mara; the door closes behind him.

The apartment is empty.

The stereo is still playing. It is very loud.

SUBJECTS

The Art of Living

You once slept with Ronna, who slept with Brian, who on successive nights slept with two girls named Vicky, one of whom was bisexual. The other Vicky, the one who was not bisexual, slept with Alan in Israel; they were on their first trip away from home and it was the first time for either of them. Alan slept with Avis, and so did his identical-twin brother Carl, and Avis slept with Scott, and Scott gave Elspeth nonspecific urethritis. Elspeth slept with Jerry a couple of times while she was engaged to him, and Jerry slept with Shelli, whom he married before he turned gay. Shelli slept with you nineteen times. Shelli has also slept with Brian, after her divorce, and with one of the Vickys while she was married. You wanted to sleep with Avis at one time but couldn't bring yourself to tell her so, and you were impotent with one of the Vickys, and now you pretend you can't remember with which one. Jerry slept with seventy-three men in one summer and Ronna has orgasms in her sleep and Scott never masturbates. Avis has gone to live with someone whom she tells you is much better in bed than Carl or Scott or Alan, especially Alan. Elspeth had to get an abortion because she didn't know which of two married policemen was the father, and they took Shelli's last lover to the insane asylum after he broke the toilet seat. Brian and Ronna now say they are just good friends and neither of the Vickys speak to Avis anymore, although the bisexual one still has fantasies about her. Jerry once approached Carl but was turned down and Alan spent an entire half-hour staring at Ronna's breasts, the breasts you touched on the one occasion when you slept with Ronna.

You go to visit your grandmother in the hospital. The week before she took a turn for the worse. Her bladder stopped functioning; the uremic acid went through her body and put her system into shock; she was clinically dead for several minutes.

When you arrive at your grandmother's room on the seventeenth floor of the hospital, her bed is empty. She is in a wheelchair near the window, looking out at the Queensboro Bridge.

"Grandmother," you say, sounding pleased. "I didn't expect to see you out of bed."

She turns around very slowly. She is still hooked up to the intravenous and there is a bag filling with urine at her side. "Darling," your grandmother tells you, "You didn't expect to see me *at all*."

And then she says: "Everything happens to me."

The nurse, a Miss Murphy, comes in with some pills. "You're a lot better off than you were a week ago, dearie," she tells your grandmother. "Believe you me."

There is lamb fricassee for lunch. Miss Murphy gives you a bite to taste and it is good.

"Your grandmother's been complaining all morning," Miss Murphy says.

"I'm very depressed," your grandmother tells you. A piece of lamb fricassee drops from her lips.

"Eat, don't talk," Miss Murphy tells your grandmother. "Neatness counts."

In the next room you can hear people talking about you.

"He's a real prick," somebody says.

You can hear another person nodding.

A third person says, "I can't feel anything for him. I just can't feel anything for him."

If they were more poetic, they would say you have become as cold and hard as the Wisconsin winter, or as mean as Robert Frost, or as arrogant and pompous as the worst of the Borgias.

What can you do when people feel this way? You can purse your lips, for one thing. You can resolve to become colder and harder and meaner and more arrogant and pompous than ever before. You can toy with the possibility of going back to becoming a nice individual, someone who is always well liked.

But you think to yourself. And you come up with the conclusion that you are naturally neither lovable nor likable and so it is useless to pretend to be. There are more important things for you to worry about, such as getting things done. So you turn on an easy-listening radio station and it drowns out the people in the next room. And you get back to your work.

In your fantasies you are taking a walk with one of the Vickys.

"Remember when we took Classics together?" Vicky asks you.

"Uh-huh," you say. That was before you were lovers.

"I used to wonder how come you never sweated," she says. "You always looked so neat, the whole summer."

You shrug your shoulders.

"When I was absent and the teacher gave back the test papers, you took mine and lost it somewhere," Vicky reminds you.

"I was so upset," you say. "I still can't understand how I lost it. It must've been at the pizzeria."

"At least you remembered the mark," she says. "And you offered to take me to dinner to make it up to me. I couldn't believe how you were stuttering like that."

You grab Vicky's hand more tightly. "I even had to talk to my psychologist," you tell her.

"All through that term," Vicky says, looking away, "you reminded me of Hector. In the *Iliad.* Don't ask me why."

So you don't ask her why.

You kiss her instead. And then you make out the way people did in the days when it was acceptable to make out and fog up car windows and sit through movies and not see them and squirm till you ached and then go home and have the most terrific dreams.

Of course this is all a fantasy.

You are translating a difficult text into English. It is a very wearisome task, but you have finally come to the last sentence of the text. *Me sentio agape,* the sentence reads. A complex simple sentence it is, but you figure it out fairly easily. The *me* is the Spanish reflexive pronoun; it means "myself." The *sentio* is Latin for "I feel." And the *agape* is a Greek word meaning a kind of love, what kind you are not certain. You string the translation together and you come up with something like this: "I feel some kind of love for myself." A curious sentence, one making you feel the slightest bit afraid. And then the inevitable happens: you wake up. It is three o'clock in the morning and outside your window it is snowing like hell.

When you say you want to go outside, Brian tells you you are crazy.

When you open the refrigerator, Ronna says you are getting fat.

When you come downstairs, Carl tells you you are making too much noise.

When you cry, Shelli says that men don't cry.

When you get angry, Scott says that it isn't nice.

When you look at him, Jerry says your face has pimples on it.

When you sleep, Vicky says that you snore.

When you try to do work, Alan tells you that you're messing up.

When you say you feel sick, Avis says don't be a baby.

And when you talk about your dream, Elspeth says you are sick.

Everyone agrees that you cannot handle your own life.

Do not think that you do not like your life. Everyone says that you are fond of it in a comfortable, grudging way. But something is wrong with the way you live it. Jerry says you should take it as a joke. Shelli says you should be more persistent. Avis tells you to rely on others less, and Elspeth says not to try to be so independent. Alan wants you to be warmer and Carl thinks you should make more of an effort to be friendly. Scott tells you to get out more and Ronna suggests more psychotherapy. Brian says you might consider suicide. One of the Vickys, one of the real, non-fantasy Vickys, brings you books by Dale Carnegie and Norman Vincent Peale. You read them, cynically at first, but then they begin to make sense. You take a few deep breaths, you look yourself in the mirror, you dress neatly and wash your face. You puff out your chest, rub hands together vigorously, and once again you are you. Whoever that may be. And you go downstairs, prepared to face the news that your grandmother has died again.

Garibaldi in Exile

I AM ON THE FERRY, nearing the Island. A Pakistani in double-knits keeps rubbing against me. That is really the lowest.

I get up my nerve. "Your Khyber pass isn't working," I tell him.

He smiles at me. Perhaps what I said means "I like you" in Urdu. He keeps rubbing against me. We are on the prow of the ferry. We are almost there.

I grab his glasses and throw them into the water.

He doesn't say anything, and just walks away.

A few people start applauding.

The grandmothernappings on the Island have stopped. The police have caught the ringleader, Grandma Gussie Shapiro. She and several other octogenarian ladies staged their own kidnappings. They had been feigning senility for years.

Grandma Gussie's eighteen demands were unconditional. John watched her arrest on the news. She was unrepentant.

John was angry. "The woman's temerity is only exceeded by her commitment to a strong Israeli defense posture," he said.

The Albanians always take the same ferry, the 7:20 in the morning and the 6:05 at night.

Aida was angry with John. He had missed her pumpkin party.

"I'm sorry," he told her. "It's just that I was working on my wall last night. I had my tools out and lost track of the time."

"Don't hand me that shit," Aida said.

"What can I tell you," John said. "It's the age-old story: boy meets drill."

"No, it's not," Aida said. "It's because I'm fat."

Professor Bennett said that he used to live here but that he doesn't anymore. Mrs. Brown asked him why.

"The man who lived upstairs from me wanted to kill me," he said. "He thought I was trying to take away his wife."

Mrs. Brown smiled. "Where did you take her?"

"Where did I take *him,* you mean," said Professor Bennett.

Mrs. Brown was confused. "What do you mean?"

"Oh," said Professor Bennett drily. "I thought you were referring to Freud's theory of homosexual paranoia."

This used to be known as Cuckoldstown.

"What are you doing this weekend?" I asked my thesis adviser. We were in the cafeteria, looking out at Borough Hall. The clock on top of Borough Hall struck five.

"I think I'm going to rewrite *Moby Dick,*" he sighed. "From the point of view of the whale."

April has been in the movement for years. She now heads the Attica Brigade.

I love her, but I'm afraid to tell her for fear that she wouldn't sleep with me anymore.

She is taller than I am, but that doesn't bother me.

She bleaches her mustache but it's very slight to begin with. I think those sparse blonde hairs are so cute.

Even her feet are cute. She wears thongs around the house. I could eat her up.

Thirty thousand lusty Hessian mercenaries stayed here, and hardly complained.

The Borough President has a mole. No one knows where it is. He also has a reserved parking space. The parking space is on Stuyvesant Place.

John sometimes parks the Dodge there. He gets tickets and never pays them. He pastes them into a scrapbook. After all, it's not his car.

My thesis adviser and I make up jokes about D. H. Lawrence. We plan to put out a *D. H. Lawrence Jokebook.*

Question: How often did Lawrence screw Frieda?

Answer: Every seven days. Lawrence loved Frieda Weekly.

The eye doctor to the literati lived here. He treated Longfellow.

Aida and I got stoned on the boardwalk at South Beach. She showed me her love letters. One was from Felix Cavalieri. Another was from Elton John. A third was from Elton John's manager, and the last was from Donovan.

"I can't live without you," wrote Felix Cavalieri.

"I'm nothing without you, love," wrote Elton John.

"Aida, you're a real blast," wrote Elton John's manager.

Donovan was more direct. "I love you," he wrote.

They were all in the same handwriting.

Wild Bill Baumgarten invited Dr. Crocker, the noted physicist, to speak at the college. He says he is the president, he can invite anyone.

Dr. Crocker believes that black people are, by heredity, intellectually inferior to white people.

April is leading the protest. They will not let Dr. Crocker speak.

John and others are blowing whistles and clapping their hands.

No one can hear Dr. Crocker.

"Crocker shit, Crocker shit," chants Aida.

No one can hear Dr. Crocker.

"No First Amendment for racists," shouts the Pakistani from the ferry. He is squinting.

A free-for-all erupts.

In the old days, abolitionists had a hard time protecting their homes.

Disturbances keep breaking out. Dean O'Hanlon is in the elevator, rushing somewhere. Another meeting. She is out of breath and tired.

"Why am I doing this?" she says, to no one in particular. "I could be somebody's grandmother."

She thinks for a moment, catches her breath. "I *am* somebody's grandmother," she says.

Her floor arrives and she rushes to the meeting.

April claims to be going through a retroactive nervous breakdown. She says she had it last December, and just didn't know it. She realizes it only now.

It depresses her that she missed out on it. That's why she should be in therapy, I tell her.

Garibaldi was restless here. He made candles and shot thrushes to pass the time.

"It's a funny thing how reputations get started here," Professor Bennett said. "I find I now have this reputation for being an aficionado."

"An aficionado?" asked Mrs. Brown.

"Whips, my dear," Professor Bennett said. "You see, one day some years ago, a student of mine, a young man taking my Metaphysical Poets course, gave me a whip as a gift. I appreciated the gift—he had gotten it in South America somewhere.

"One day a girl in the same class, a girl who rarely showed up for class and was failing because of that, came to my office. The poor girl was in tears, and said, 'Professor Bennett, isn't there *anything* I can do to pass your course?'

"So I cracked the whip, rather deftly and with a grand gesture, and said, 'Are you handy with one of these, my dear?'

"She ran out of the office screaming."

"Oh, my," said Mrs. Brown, laughing.

"It was a harmless little thing, actually," Professor Bennett said. "Rather like the young man who gave it to me."

John works for DeJoy. He drives a car for him. We have no taxicabs here, just private car services.

An Oriental woman got off the ferry once and got into John's car. She asked him to take her to the Tibetan Museum. When they got there, she told John to wait outside for her to return. John waited for three hours, but she didn't come out.

John radioed DeJoy and asked him what to do.

"If yuh don't wanna be a fucking doormat," DeJoy said, "Don't lay down in front of the fucking door."

The streets here bear the names of Presidential candidates of the Prohibition Party: Bidwell, Wooley and Fiske.

April has a recurring dream. In the dream, she is running on all fours, on her hands and knees, just like a dog.

"It's so exhilarating," she tells me. "I go faster than I could using just my feet. I make fantastic time. I run the length of Hylan Boulevard in fifteen minutes."

What does it mean, though? I ask her. What does being on all fours mean to her?

"I haven't the slightest idea," she says. "But I hope it always means the same thing."

We were sitting in Montezuma's Revenge, John, April, Aida and I. We were eating enchiladas.

Aida took out a Flair and began writing on her napkin. She handed it to April, who read it and put it down. John was explaining Keynesian theory to me.

When I returned to the table alone later, to put down the tip, I read the napkin.

"If I don't get my friend next month," it said, "guess who's going to be in big trouble."

Our cicada collection is one of the largest in the world.

Teenyboppers and hitters line the shopping mall. I am afraid of them. I can't tell them apart. A teenybopper girl (or is she a hitter?) comes up to me, wearing platforms, chewing gum. I freeze.

She looks disappointed.

"Shit," she says. "You looked like John Denver. But only for a minute."

I apologize to her.

It's late at night. Aida is standing on top of Todt Hill. The view is justly famous. She contemplates suicide.

"I am a delicate flower," she tells herself.

"I need to be watered."

"But I just can't find the right gardeners," she says aloud.

She begins to cry.

There is another place with the same name. It is near the Straits of Magellan. There are penguins there. We have none.

April will not take the ferry. She says it makes her seasick.

"Every morning when I get up," she tells Aida, "I thank God for Othmar Ammann."

"Who," Aida asks, "is Othmar Ammann?"

"Without him," April says, "I couldn't get off this fucking island."

My thesis adviser has refused tenure. He has written Wild Bill Baumgarten to that effect. He says he doesn't want to have an unfair advantage over his colleagues who haven't published much.

My thesis adviser is the author of two books, *Subtle Kinship: John Middleton Murry and Katherine Mansfield* and *From Dionysius to Despotism.*

Professor Bennett has written three books, all about George Herbert.

Wild Bill Baumgarten has written a book about higher education, *Something for Everyone Isn't Much.*

Dr. Crocker has a book out now, a best seller. I can't remember the name of it.

Dean O'Hanlon has written a textbook, *Quantum Chemistry,* in two volumes.

John is the author of a book extolling Vitamin E. It is published by a vanity house and is called *The Love Song of D-Alpha Tocopherol.*

April doesn't want to write a book. Neither does DeJoy or Mrs. Brown, or the Pakistani.

Aida is almost finished with her novel. It is to be titled *Scenes from a Mirage.* I hear it is autobiographical.

I have been working on my thesis for two and a half years. I don't do much else. Somehow I cannot bring myself to complete it.

I'm always aware that I'm on an island. It must be strange not to live on one.

Au Milieu Intérieur

What is a dream?

He was in the city, but it was his own block. And she was in his house. Outside she pointed to his car in the driveway; two other cars had parked too close to the yellow lines on the sidewalk, and it would be difficult for him to remove his car. He was afraid, but he got into the car, and she showed him that he had plenty of room. Suddenly she began to point out an airplane that was coming in for a landing, and he became annoyed with her for distracting him during such a difficult maneuver. Yet somehow he managed to get the car out of the driveway even while watching the airplane land. And then she disappeared, so apparently he would be allowed to go home.

What is a dream?

He was driving, and had to urinate. So when the pressure on his bladder became unbearable, he stopped off at a carnival to look for a bathroom. But when he got out of the car, he discovered that it had been a false alarm, merely the pressure of the car's seat belt on his groin. At the carnival, a clown was entertaining a group of small children. The clown kept blowing up a balloon, bigger and bigger. He would say, "Shall I do it more?" after each blow; the children were delighted. "More! More!" they squealed. Eventually, of course, the balloon burst.

He had been expecting it, yet the loud noise startled him anyway. On the way out of the carnival, he ran into his uncle, who had gotten so much older.

How does it feel to be a man?

When he was ten years old and sitting poolside at a San Juan hotel, he called a woman an adultress. She was a redhaired secretary from Cleveland, sunning herself in a brown bikini. She told him that one day someone would punch him in the nose. He protested that an adultress was merely a female adult, just as a poetess was a female poet. But he knew it went beyond that; how far, he wasn't sure. He was scared of the pink flamingos which chased him across the hotel grounds, and he was even more terrified by the naked children shouting, "Americano! Americano!" as his parents threw pennies from the taxi. And in El Morro castle, he was worried that he might fall through one of the holes in the floor. The guide had said that Ponce de León once fell through one of the holes and thus discovered Florida.

What is an anxiety attack?

One evening, while baking carrot cake, he realized that he always cringed inwardly when his mother approached, knowing that there was something he was doing wrong: either sitting down incorrectly so that he was damaging the back of the car, or getting powder in the cracks of the tiles of the bathroom floor, or else getting a stain on the carpeting, a stain invisible to everyone but his mother. His mother had believed in a sterilized world and an antiseptic, well-thought-out life, and for a long time he believed that it was the only kind of life available to him.

Once he found out differently, he was furious for what he had missed. And while it made him doubt his own reality, he learned after awhile to appreciate the possibilities. Eventually he stopped listening to his mother. When she talked about something, he would imagine her an inmate in a mental institution, screaming insane, irrational things out from behind bars. In the long run, it made things easier.

Why do people have to die?

In the 1950s there was a television serial he watched when he came home from school for peanut butter and jelly. The show was called "Love of Life." Every day, the program would begin with a deep-voiced announcer announcing: " 'Love of Life': Vanessa Dale's Search for Human Dignity."

He wondered if it had become impossible to live with dignity. There were long lines everywhere: at the movies, in banks, at gasoline stations. On the subways people were cattle, herded from one malfunctioning train to another by transit cowboys disguised as policemen. All over the West Side he was treated like a messenger, and hence as less than human. Behind all those precise, lower-case graphics and shag carpeting and Danish modern glass partitions there was a machine, a machine with people for parts. At five o'clock the machine became a monster and vomited up the day's food. He was quite nearly a part of that vomit.

What is a dream?

For years he was obsessed with vomiting. While nobody he knew thought the process was charming, no one but he seemed to realize the extent of its horror. Every day he would become nauseated to the point of vomiting. Every day he would sit and sweat and put things in his mouth and write out secret codes on notebook looseleaf paper. "NNN" meant "No Nausea Now."

"LMBOK" stood for "Let Me Be Okay." "DGPNVT" was shorthand for "Dear God Please No Vomiting Today."

Once he came very close to vomiting. It was in high school, in a Social Studies class. He sat next to a girl whose eyes bulged out of their sockets; he assumed she had some kind of condition, but her eyes were robin's-egg blue and the overall effect was not unattractive. When the teacher told the class that President Harding had had VD, the girl wanted to know what VD was, and she almost seemed to believe the teacher's smiling explanation that the initials stood for Valentine's Day. But that day he could stand the onrushing wave of nausea no longer, and involuntarily he moaned, "Oh, I'm gonna throw up . . ." The girl with the bulging eyes became agitated and jumped up from her seat (they sat in the middle two rows and their seats were attached) and she cried out to the class: "He's sick! He's sick!"

Three years later, when he was able to use public transportation again, he saw the girl on a bus. Evidently she had married, for she carried a baby in her arms.

How can people live like that?

On the back of the photograph she had written in a small, neat handwriting: "Well, we went through a lot together, but I think we finally understand each other. I know I'll always remember you and what we went through together. I hope you will, too, and whenever you look at this picture, you'll remember only the good times."

Where does it hurt?

He called her, crying hysterically, great heaving sobs. She told him she could not make out the words and that he should calm down and try to tell her exactly what had happened. He took deep breaths and finally related the story of the unprotected eggs and the muttered obscenities and the hollering and the lost appetite and the threats and the mess and the scorned tears and the cry, "But I love you!" going unheard. He knew he was powerless, he said. When he finished the story, she told him, "You need to know someone cares." He agreed, but said he needed to know more; he needed to know he was not crazy. She told him there must be a reason why he was so affected, and he, being rational before she could say it, said, "The telephone is not the best place to discuss these things. I'll see you at the usual time on Tuesday." And he hung up the receiver, looked in the mirror, watched himself sob, his face and eyes red and swollen, his stomach rebelling, and he thought: Well, at least I've cleaned out my sinuses.

How does it feel to be alone?

He was almost surprised that he had survived the night. It had hardly bothered him at all, having only himself for company. He drank jasmine tea and dipped into Proust, and after a while he looked up from his book and the digital clock read 11:47. So he put on the flannel bathrobe and went to the kitchen and watched the poor fools in Times Square and the older, more affluent fools dancing to Guy Lombardo's gray hotel music. To him it was absurd: cheering a new year, applauding the passage of time. One might just as well celebrate the movement of a glacier.

He settled down to sleep at about 1 A.M., only to awaken two hours later when the telephone rang. No one spoke, so he just said, "Happy New Year," and he hung up the receiver. Within five minutes he was asleep again.

What should a person do?

On the way to her house, he felt nauseated. When he realized that the nausea was anger, he found himself becoming furious. He walked in and immediately proceeded to tell her how damned sick he was of her controlling his life, of his jumping at her every command. He had fantasies of torturing her, he said, using the toilet seat.

She was silent. Then she asked, "Why?"

"Damn you," he said. "I'm angry because you're so fucking important to me."

He gave her a very hard time, waiting for her to become angry, waiting for her to become hurt. But he knew he was afraid to hurt her, because he had made her a goddess, and if she cried because of him, his image of her would be shattered. Then there would be no order in the galaxy.

Afterwards he felt ashamed.

How does it feel to be a man?

For a long time he wanted a black eye. The thought of physical violence excited him only when it would result in his getting a black eye. He kept hoping to get into a fight, a fight in which a stronger opponent would punch him squarely and surely in the eye. Although he took to hanging out in tough neighborhoods, and though he sometimes shoved people in the street, he never did meet anyone who would fight with him, and he was sorely disappointed. He had to resort to artificial black eyes, those made from carbon paper or mascara or India ink.

Eventually he became close enough to another person to ask for a black eye. But almost as soon as he got the words out, the desire had disappeared. A black eye was no longer necessary.

What should a person do?

He was taught that one way to relieve tension was to have a knock-down, drag-out argument at home so that he could appear calm in public, in society. So it was natural, perhaps, that when he first began to see her, he would pick a quarrel before he went out. Yet when he had the presence of mind to ask others if something was bothering them, he got a look of almost pitying puzzlement. Why, they wondered, would he bring up *feelings* when someone's cufflinks were missing? He remembered his father telling the first psychiatrist that the best thing to do sometimes was to repress a thing that upset you. It was a not untypical response from an American male with ulcers.

What is a dream?

Coming over the bridge in the evening, he saw the moon directly between two cables. It was a mustard-colored moon, partially covered by low-hanging gray-blue clouds.

What should a person do?

He was told, "The world, after all, is a large place . . . ." And he grudgingly admitted that perhaps he wanted to know her intimately, that he wanted to know all facets of her. He was told that he was interested in knowing people and experiencing them in many ways. Why, then, she asked, did he limit himself to one person, and at that, a person who would not be completely his. He protested, "Do you mean that it's not really *love?*" and she said that it was not necessary to assume she was taking away the anchors from his life; she was merely raising questions. Bitterly, he said, "Well, excuse me, I thought that I was enjoying myself on Saturday. Now tell me I was mistaken." She did not respond to his challenge, but said instead:

"You want to be a baby, neither a man nor a woman. You have a fear of losing control during orgasm. You are scared of losing some part of you, a vital creative essence, along with the loss of semen. Even though others acknowledge your manhood, even though it comes from the person from whom you want it most, this does not satisfy you. For it does not come from within."

He said that it scared him to even think about it. She smiled. "That's a different problem," she said.

When do people become happy?

Someone told him: "You may think that you're unstable and fragile and insecure, but I'll tell you, kid, when it comes to other people you're a brick."

He was a brick.

How does it feel to be with someone?

He was desperate. Finally he said into the receiver, "It's just that you get into the habit of loving."

"But is that love?" she asked. And before he could respond, she excused herself from the telephone. It was characteristic of her; she said that her brother had been calling her.

Years later, at parties, she would tell people that they had been together for two years. He would laugh and correct her and say, "It was only a year, eleven months, two weeks and three days." And she would laugh, and look at him, and take his hand, an old friend's hand.

Why do people have to die?

He was reading the sports section of the newspaper. A story about a football game. The quarterback had to leave the game at halftime; he received a telephone call saying that his father had died. The team was defeated, 21–16. The coach of the team was quoted, in speaking of the quarterback, "His loss was greater than ours."

He put down the newspaper, wondering what to do next.

What should a person do?

He was called in as a consultant on a very difficult, very similar case. A ten-year-old boy who was afraid to go to a basketball game in Madison Square Garden. The boy was afraid he would get sick there.

The father asked him for advice. He told the father, "Force him to go. Otherwise it will only become worse in the future. He will avoid going places until finally he won't go out at all." He was sure of his diagnosis.

When he went in, he found the boy in a familiar state: pacing, crying, overbreathing. "I'm having a nervous breakdown," the ten-year-old said.

He told the boy that one must do the things that were frightening. The boy still cried, and the father slapped the boy, saying, "Listen to this man! He's the voice of experience."

He told the boy that he really wanted to go out, that he loved basketball. He said it would be hell and then asked, "Who ever said it was going to be easy?"

After half an hour of talking, he convinced the boy to go. The father was very grateful; he called the next day to say that all had gone well, that they were only sorry that the home team had lost.

It was the satisfaction he needed, the confirmation of what he had just begun to suspect: that he was a success.

What is a dream?

He was half-asleep when the telephone rang. "Are you awake?" the caller asked.

"No, I'm a funeral," he said, smiling dreamily.

And then there were widowers. Widowers flying everywhere.

The Mother in My Bedroom

My mother is in my bedroom, lying underneath my bed. On top of the bed my pseudonymous girlfriend Sarah Lawrence of Arabia and I are making love. We are doing it in the missionary position, momma/poppa style. Every time we hump we depress the mattress and my mother gets hit in the head. She does not get hit hard enough for her to get a headache.

Sarah Lawrence of Arabia keeps having orgasms. Five are not enough for her. She keeps wanting to have more.

"Let him have *his* orgasm already," my mother mutters from under the bed. Luckily Sarah Lawrence of Arabia is too involved in her passion to hear my mother.

Finally I am allowed to have my orgasm and it is a fairly good one, as good as Sarah Lawrence of Arabia's fourth. She is very jealous of this; I try to pretend it was only a so-so orgasm, but she can tell how good it was from my eyes.

Sarah Lawrence of Arabia puts on her veil and gets dressed. My mother comes out from the bed to help her with her clothes.

"Do you really love my son?" my mother asks her as she hands her an Yves St. Laurent scarf.

Sarah Lawrence of Arabia says, "Yes, I do."

My mother isn't satisfied with this. "But do you love his pee, his farts, his shit, his huge cock?" My mother has been reading Erica Jong.

Sarah Lawrence of Arabia adjusts her veil and her scarf so they do not get in each other's way. She walks out of my room without saying anything.

I sit on the rug and watch my mother change the sheets. "I hear retarded girls make the best wives," she tells me.

My mother is in my bedroom. She is cleaning again, this time with the help of Bernice, our black cleaning woman. Bernice comes in every other day. On Wednesdays Bernice does my room under my mother's supervision. Usually I am out but this Wednesday I am in bed with a cold.

Bernice and my mother make my bed with me still in it. I am reading the Living Section of *The New York Times* and drinking fennel tea.

"Did you ever hear that retarded girls make the best wives, Bernice?" my mother asks.

Bernice nods. She cannot speak. She is smoking a Now. They have only 0.2 milligrams "tar."

I shake my head. "Mother, leave Bernice alone. She's not interested in such things."

"*Of course* she's interested," my mother says. She is dusting my books. She sees a book's title, *Physical Education,* opens it, and looks dismayed when she realizes it is an old college textbook.

Bernice begins vacuuming. I am sipping my fennel tea and trying to read an article about Cuisinarts. My mother keeps coming over to see what I'm reading. I deliberately try to hide the page from her.

"You know, Bernice," my mother says, "Some people must have guilty consciences."

Bernice opens her mouth. I know if she could make sounds she would be laughing.

Bernice moves the bed so she can vacuum under it. I start to roll toward my bookcase. My mother likes it to be clean under the bed.

My mother is in my bedroom, watching a violent TV show. A son gets hit by his mother again and again and again. Ann Sothern is playing the mother in the show and she is really beating up her son.

"This is incredible," my mother says to me.

I am sitting in my rocking chair, necking casually with Sarah Lawrence of Arabia. She smells like a deodorant soap.

Ann Sothern keeps slapping, hitting, pummeling her son.

"Can you imagine this, a mother hitting her own son like that?" my mother cries. "Why, he's running out of cheeks to turn!"

Sarah Lawrence of Arabia gives my mother a disgusted look. My mother is too involved with the TV show to see it.

I put my tongue in Sarah Lawrence of Arabia's mouth. She begins to get aroused and we move onto the bed. "Oh no, just at the best part," my mother sighs. She shuts off the TV with the remote control device and crawls under the bed.

My mother is in my bedroom. She and Bernice are showing it to Bernice's Indian grandmother, Lahoma, who is visiting from Virginia. Grandma Lahoma teaches Judaic Studies at William and Mary. She believes herself to be descended from the Ten Lost Tribes.

Bernice points to my bed. "Very nicely made," her grandmother says. Bernice smiles proudly.

"My son has a lot of books," my mother tells our guest. "Bernice and I have a difficult job dusting them all."

Grandma Lahoma looks thoughtful. Her braids are grey. She is wearing a *chai.*

"He reads a lot of poetry, mostly," my mother says. "I don't understand poetry that doesn't rhyme. I was brought up on Edgar Allan Poe."

Grandma Lahoma takes out a book from the bookshelf, clears her throat. "William Carlos Williams," she says. Bernice nods her head vigorously. She likes dusting poetry books the best.

"My son *writes* poetry, too," my mother says. She takes out a piece of yellow legal paper from my night-table drawer. "Listen to this," she tells them, and she begins reading: " 'I feel drowned in this place. I can no longer control my dizzying, boundless, sometimes terrifying openness to experience more things than this . . . .' "

Bernice shakes her head, takes a long drag on her Now.

"Probably just a phase," Grandma Lahoma assures my mother. Then they start talking about Israel.

My mother comes in my bedroom. She has news for me.

"The House has just passed and sent to the Senate a 125 billion-dollar defense budget." She is quite out of breath from rushing up the stairs.

"I don't care," I tell her.

"What's that you're doing?"

"Packing."

"Don't be silly." Unconsciously she begins straightening out my bookshelves.

"I'm leaving," I say, apparently with some firmness in my voice.

My mother blinks. "Don't be pragmatic," she says. She is using the wrong adjective and she knows it. "Don't be silly," she says again, this time more sure of the word.

"Goodbye," I say, my hand on the doorknob. "I'm leaving you most of my books. Bernice can have the poetry."

Near the front end of my mother's brain stem, in the diencephalon, are the centers for anger, rage, and pain. From looking at her I can see that these centers are activating themselves.

I leave before I can see anything further.

On the porch I can hear things breaking. "Damn that Arab slut!" my mother is screaming. I hurry away in my Datsun B-210.

My mother is in my bedroom. She won't come out of it now. Bernice has to come in every day and bring my mother her meals. Some workmen are installing a toilet and sink where my rocking chair used to be. Downstairs a young black girl is giving her baby a bottle. Bernice appears to be in charge of things now.

We correspond almost daily. She, too, is trying to write poetry, but she knows she is only an amateur. Bernice has to look after my mother now, and she is philosophical about it.

"In the end we are all amateurs," Bernice writes. "Progress is our most important poet."

ARTIFACTS

The Finest Joe Colletti Story Ever Written (so far)

FOR JOE COLLETTI, today is always the present, sometimes the future, often the past.

How's that for an opening sentence? There are so many good ones I could use. I want to make it really a socko beginning for my Joe Colletti story. Joe deserves only the best. It's a pity I can't use all my possible opening sentences in this story. Here are a couple of others I thought up:

The world is a closer place, and Joe Colletti is part of it.

"It looks like a penis, only smaller," Joe Colletti said to the man who exposed himself.

Joe Colletti is the only one for me.

I can't believe I'm so lucky as to actually be writing a story about Joe Colletti. It's a real honor. I can't for the life of me understand why anybody would want to write a story about any other character. Surely there is no one worth writing about as much as Joe Colletti.

What people are saying about Joe Colletti . . .

Stella Maris, Richmond, Virginia: "There are people in this world . . . and then there is Joe Colletti."

Hyman Peckeroff, The Bronx, New York: "Of all the Joe Collettis in the world, he's certainly the Joe Colletti-est."

Virginia Plight, Atlanta, Georgia: "Joe Colletti takes his initials seriously."

I'm really not sure I'm up to the task of writing a story about a man like Joe Colletti. Consider my next paragraph:

Joe Colletti utters the most profound statement ever made. People swoon as soon as he is finished with his last syllable. It is the ultimate finale for most of the women in the audience. The men are crying openly. There are halos over each infant in his crib. Joe Colletti looks better, at this moment, than any other person in history has ever looked. Nothing can compare with Joe Colletti and with that everyone will agree.

See? That doesn't make it. It's hard to get into words what I feel about Joe Colletti. There are people who say no one should even *attempt* to write stories about Joe Colletti. Yet that doesn't stop people from trying. Everyone has his own special vision of Joe. But on paper, it all looks so puny and insignificant. How does one communicate the utter——of Joe Colletti. (Notice: there is no descriptive noun in the English language that will even suffice in this case.)

What makes Joe Colletti Joe Colletti? Does anyone know? Come on, you guys, please help me out. Why are you just sitting around reading this? Let's get some dialogue going between us here: that's the way Joe Colletti would want it. You're the reader of this Joe Colletti story. I'm the writer. Let's have some communication already. This is a two-way street, you know. Here's a blank space for *you* to fill in with your favorite anecdote about Joe Colletti. Come on, it's easy once you start. Anyone who knows even the *slightest* thing about Joe Colletti (and that includes 99.999% of the human race) can do it. Just try. Please, for me and more importantly, for Joe Colletti. A better Joe Colletti story is up to you.

See? It wasn't that hard, was it? I'm sure any one of you could write your own Joe Colletti story if you wanted to. The problem is most of you are too lazy to try. Oh, you may have more talent than me; I don't deny that. I don't have much natural talent for this sort of thing; I'm not a congenital writer of Joe Colletti stories. But talent is cheap, as Joe himself keeps reminding us. You've got to use your talent or it will atrophy, just like Joe Colletti's grandmother's pinky ring. I've seen thousands of people with talent, but they never got anywhere. You know why? Because they didn't have that *will to succeed* that Joe Colletti has, that same *will to succeed* that I am trying to emulate here.

Every night for two months I've been saying to myself before I went to bed: "You *will* write the best Joe Colletti story ever written.... You *will* write the best Joe Colletti story ever written...." I dare you to write a better Joe Colletti story than this one. If you succeed, I will rejoice with you. Joe Colletti deserves only the best. For now I believe this story is the best one, and that it supersedes and outdates every previous Joe Colletti story, including the one by John Updike.

"Take Joe Colletti . . . please."
"Screw Joe Colletti."
"I do!"
"So do I!"
"Boy, everyone's into Joe Colletti these days . . . . Or is it the other way around?"
(Overheard by me on an Eastern Airlines WhisperJet.)

This is a test from the Emergency Fiction System. This is only a test.
MMMMMMMMMMMMMMMMMMMMMMMMMMMMMM mmmmmmmmmmmmmmmmmmmmmmmmmmmmm MMMMM MMMMMMMMMMMMMMM mmmmmmmmmmmmmmmmm.
The preceding was a test from the Emergency Fiction System. The fiction writers in your area, in cooperation with the federal government, have agreed to include this test, designed by Joe Colletti, in their stories. This was only a test. Had this been an actual emergency, Joe Colletti would have interrupted this story and told you where to turn for emergency information and assistance. This ends this test from the Emergency Fiction System.

"   ," Joe Colletti is saying. He has been hitchhiking in the Arizona desert. He is dressed inconspicuously. He has just gotten a lift with a Mercury Comet, '72, gold with a brown vinyl top.

The driver of the car is a thick-lipped woman in her fifties with a voracious Russian accent. She stares at Joe Colletti as she drives. Finally she says to him:

"My father, you know, was a world-famous Soviet dictator . . . . He sent thousands to their deaths and behaved very cruelly in persecuting various minority group members."

"   ," Joe Colletti responds. "

          ?"

"My mother was the Indiana Safe Driving Day Poster Girl of 1927," the woman says. "I came to this country only a few years ago after a life of torment abroad. At first the American people took to me in that same publicized, half-hearted way that they embraced various astronauts. . . . I was inundated with vaguely flatulent bubbles of faint praise."

"

          ," Joe Colletti tells her.

"Why, yes . . . I *do* feel like that sometimes," the woman driver says. "Thank you, young man, for making everything so clear to me. It's as though a veil has been lifted from my eyes." The woman looks towards Joe Colletti with deep gratitude in her Slavic eyes. "How can I ever repay you?" she asks.

"   ," Joe Colletti says, and the Russian woman driver begins to smile the biggest smile she has ever smiled.

I'm crying now. I hate to be like Charles Dickens or Erich Segal and cry while I'm writing my own stories, but that anecdote about Joe Colletti and that Russian woman always breaks me up. Those of you who have heard it before, don't you agree that no one has rendered that scene as deftly as I did? Wasn't that a master stroke, leaving Joe's dialogue blank? I, unlike so many previous Joe Colletti story writers, know my limitations. That's why this is the best Joe Colletti story ever written. I do not attempt to tamper with the higher things. There are some who do. In one recent story by a writer who will here remain nameless (although he is a lowly skunk), a character foolishly named Wanda Wetherbee says: "Joe Colletti isn't *really* Joe Colletti, and you can't get me to believe that!" I see no sense in writing such trash. Hanging is too good for the creep who wrote that about Joe Colletti.

One thing every Joe Colletti story needs, says one scholar, is a description of Joe Colletti: "Each Colletti tale from time immemorial has always included a woefully inadequate description of Joe," the scholar writes. "This is crucial to the genre." Not wishing to break a literary tradition going back to Joe-Colletti-knows-when, here is my stab at it:

Joe Colletti looks like an early photograph of someone who is older.

Short, sweet, and to the point, eh? I can feel Joe's presence beside me as this is being written.

When I was a boy and afraid of thunder, my mother would comfort me by saying, "Richard, you've got to remember that every person, from the most important on down to the lowliest beggar, wishes at some time that he or she were Joe Colletti looking elegant in a stately satin bathrobe." Then I would dry my little eyes and forget the thunder, pretending that I . . . little boy that I was . . . that *I* was the man who stole Joe Colletti's coffeecup in the famous Houston Dining Room Massacre. Such is the hold that Joe Colletti has on all little children.

I recognize that I am too incompetent a writer to end this story about Joe Colletti. Lesser writers than I have taken it upon themselves to actually devise endings for Joe Colletti stories, and that is where they have failed. There is no ending worthy of Joe Colletti. It is impossible to end this story, or *any* Joe Colletti story, and still manage to communicate the essence of Joe Collettism. Therefore, this story will have no ending, no final sentence. This last sentence is *not* the last sentence in this, the finest Joe Colletti story ever written (so far).

"But in a Thousand Other Worlds"

One morning in early April or late March of 1977, Richard Grayson, a fiction writer living in Brooklyn, completed a story titled "But in a Thousand Other Worlds." Richard was quite satisfied with this story. As he proofread it, he became more and more convinced that it was one of the best stories he had ever written. "It has everything," Richard thought. "Humor, literary playfulness, innovation, heart . . . ." He showed it to his friend Nina Mule, who immediately agreed. The only problem Nina had with the story was its unwieldly title. "I don't think the story can carry its weight," Nina told Richard over Sunday brunch at Yellowfingers.

"*Of course* it can," Richard snapped, his mouth still filled with unswallowed quiche. "The title comes from my favorite soap opera, *Another World.* When the show began in 1964, an announcer would say over the opening title: 'We do not live in this world alone, but in a thousand other worlds. . . And now, *Another World*. . .' "

"I see," said Nina, absentmindedly stirring her Bloody Mary with the celery stick. "But I'm still not sure it works."

Richard just sighed. But the story itself grew indignant. "I'm not sure *you* work," the story told Nina, who was employed in the *Wall Street Journal*'s advertising department.

Nina looked at the story in disbelief. "Well, I never . . ." she started to say.

"And your dialogue's not so hot, either," said "But in a Thousand Other Worlds." "Boy, what a cliché for surprised indignation. Can't you think up anything better than that?"

Richard was dismayed at his story. "Please," he told it. "Nina didn't mean anything by it. She's my friend, you see, and was just offering constructive criticism. You can't take these things to heart."

"Hmmpf," said the story. "What do you think I am, made of stone? I've got feelings too, you know. I'm a pretty sensitive story."

Nina smiled, trying to make amends. "Would you like some of my omelet?" she offered.

"Not on your life, sister," piped the story. "I'm on a low-cholesterol diet."

Richard looked at Nina with a helpless shrug, as if to say, "Stories will be stories." He hoped Nina, a dear old friend, would not take his story's rudeness as something he, Richard, had anything to do with. But Nina was a wise and worldly woman; she knew it was only a story talking, and not Richard himself. In college she had learned to separate the author from his work.

They took the story to see a Truffaut double bill at the Carnegie Hall Cinema, then went their separate ways. On the ride back to Brooklyn, Richard and his story did not say a word.

That evening, though, the story came over to Richard just as he was about to begin a new story at his typewriter. "But in a Thousand Other Worlds" seemed to be jealous. "Look," it said, "If you're going to start a new piece, I want to be out of here. Put me in a manila envelope and send me to *The New Yorker*."

"*The New Yorker?*" Richard smiled. "Boy, do you have delusions of grandeur!"

"Come on," insisted the story. "I can do it."

"All right," said Richard without his usual hesitation. "I'll mail you out first thing in the morning."

"*Now* you're talking," the satisfied story said. "And don't forget a stamped, self-addressed envelope . . . just in case."

Richard couldn't help smiling. In a way he loved his story. It certainly had more confidence than *he* did. "I won't forget," he promised.

Two weeks later the story came back. Attached to it was a form rejection notice with some words written underneath. "This is too much like Barthelme for our comfort," the words were.

Richard wasn't surprised, but of course he still felt a little disappointed. The story, however, was merely outraged.

"Too much like Barthelme indeed!" the story howled. "My dialogue has resonance!"

Richard didn't like the looks of the story. Its stay at *The New Yorker* had obviously had a bad effect on it. "Come on, you've got to learn to face rejection," he told the story. "It was a million-to-one chance."

The story remained silent. It sulked for most of the week, jealous of the new story Richard lavished such attention on. "But in a Thousand Other Worlds" demanded to be sent out again.

"What's the rush? Richard wanted to know. "You're not topical or anything."

"Let *me* decide that, please," the story said. "I can't stay here anymore. This place is driving me bananas. Send me anywhere, just submit me again . . ."

Impatient, Richard told the story in no uncertain terms that *he* was the writer and *he* was his own agent and the story could just sit and stew till *he* was good and ready to resubmit it elsewhere.

The story stormed out of the house, slamming the door with surprising force. Richard sighed, but he knew it would come back sooner or later.

"*Wall Street Journal,* advertising," said Nina Mule as she picked up her phone at the office.

"Ms. Mule?" asked the voice.

"Yes?"

"This is Sergeant Mulgrew at the 23rd Precinct. We've picked up a story for soliciting outside the offices of *Harper's Magazine.* The story gave your name as its author. Are you familiar with a 'But in a Thousand Other Worlds', Ms. Mule?"

"Yes," Nina said. "But I didn't write it. My friend Richard Grayson did. I read it, however, and I thought it was pretty good."

The voice on the other end of the phone coughed. "I'm a police officer, Ms. Mule, and I don't make literary value judgments. I just do my job. We're willing to drop all charges, this being a first offense and all. Will you or Mr. Grayson come down to the station house to identify the story and take it home?"

"I'll call Richard right now," said Nina.

"Damn you," Richard told his story as they walked out of the precinct house.

The story just smirked.

"Do you think this is funny?" Richard demanded. "It's damn embarrassing."

The story chuckled.

"All right," sighed Richard as they got into his car. "I'm sending you out again tonight. But not to any slick magazine, oh no. You're going to a little mag that pays in copies."

Imbecile, thought "But in a Thousand Other Worlds." I'll show you.

Richard didn't hear from the story again until August. There were other stories coming now, new ones, more innovative ones, more humorous ones, far more publishable ones. Then one morning "But in a Thousand Other Worlds" arrived in Richard's mailbox. Someone had removed its paper clip and stapled its pages together. There was a coffee stain on it.

"This story STINKS," someone had written in big printed letters on a sheaf of loose-leaf paper.

By now Richard was almost glad to see this arrogant story humbled in this way.

"What did you expect?" the story shouted. "*You* did this to me! You sent me to a magazine where they only like traditional, boring stories. When they found out I wasn't representational, they just tore me apart! And of course I stink—it's been a killer of a summer."

Despite himself, Richard felt pity for the story. "Look," he told it, "Next week I'm going to the Bread Loaf Writers' Conference. I'll take you along. That good Vermont air should have you feeling better in no time."

The story didn't say anything. But it looked resentful.

Richard had his conference with the novelist John Gardner on a drizzly Sunday morning at Bread Loaf. They were seated in the big barn, in a corner away from most people. John Gardner took out Richard's stories, placed them on his lap, and began to puff on his pipe.

John Gardner didn't think much of most of Richard's work. "You have talent, that's obvious," he told Richard. "But why you waste it on crap like this is beyond me."

Richard just nodded.

John Gardner took out "But in a Thousand Other Worlds." "*This* story in particular," John Gardner said. "To me, it's just nonsense. And it's not only nonsense, it's immoral. Immoral."

"Well . . ." Richard began. But before he could say anything else, his story bit John Gardner on the leg, very hard.

"Je-*sus!*" cried John Gardner. "I'll need a tetanus shot now! That story is a real son of a bitch!"

Dreadfully embarrassed, Richard took the next bus back to New York City. He wanted to throw the story out the window, but the Greyhound's windows were all locked shut.

Arriving at home, Richard mailed out the story to *The Atlantic Monthly* without saying a word.

It was late October when the story returned. It looked jaundiced. Richard had completely forgotten about it by then. He had had acceptances from *Shenandoah* and *The Carleton Miscellany* and was excited by this. "But in a Thousand Other Worlds" now seemed to him an embarrassment.

"This story is sick," said the scrawl over the printed rejection form.

"Bastards," the story said. "They didn't give me a chance."

Richard was about to put the story back into his files when it started crying. "Send me out again," the story pleaded. "I don't want to stay here with a man like you." And then it collapsed.

Wasting no time, Richard rushed it to the emergency room at Coney Island Hospital. The intern who looked at it took its case history from Richard. Then she rushed it into an examining room. Richard followed, but the doctor told him he couldn't come in.

"But I wrote it!" Richard cried.

The doctor tried to calm him down. "Look," she said, "this is a very sick story. It needs my full attention. Just sit down and relax."

Richard found a telephone and called Nina. She said she would come right over.

It was an hour before the doctor came out. Richard and Nina were pacing the waiting room floor.

"I'm afraid *The Atlantic Monthly* was right," said the doctor.

"We've got a very sick story on our hands."

Richard began to cry.

"What is it, Doctor?" Nina asked.

"A coronary occlusion," the doctor said.

"It *did* have a lot of heart after all," sobbed Richard.

The doctor rubbed her hands together resignedly. "Two months ago," she said, "maybe even last month . . . major rewriting could have saved it. At least it might have had a chance to make *some* little magazine. . . . But now, I'm afraid, it's hopeless . . ."

". . . It's unpublishable, then?" said Nina.

"I'm sorry."

Richard's face was buried in his hands. "I never gave it the care I should have," he said.

"Hush, now," Nina told him. "It's all over. There'll be other stories . . ."

"That's true," said Richard, wiping his eyes. "But there'll never be another 'But in a Thousand Other Worlds.' "

I never liked that title anyway, Nina thought as she helped her friend to his feet.

What *Really* Happened in Cambodia

1. The Leader

"As you can see," Pol Pot tells his visitor, "I am no Lon Nol. I am not an imperialist lackey of the American war machine. I did not come from the elite bourgeoisie. My name is not a palindrome." Pol Pot coughs. "Is that the right English word—palindrome?"

The visitor assures him that it is.

"No," says Pol Pot firmly, "palindromes are counter-revolutionary. Of course names like mine, which rhyme when they are written or spoken backwards—that is all right. Rhyming does not go against the new spirit of Kampuchea."

The visitor nods.

Pol Pot coughs, stares out the window at what once was the city of Phnom Penh. He is obviously trying to imagine what his visitor's name is backwards. The visitor knows this and it makes her uncomfortable.

Finally she asks: "Is Pol Pot your real name?" She is afraid but the question is already out of her mouth and in the Cambodian air.

Pol Pot looks at his visitor. She is bolder than he had expected. "No, Pol Pot is my revolutionary name," he tells her. "Like Stalin. Like Lenin . . ." Pol Pot seems thoughtful for a moment. "Do you think Lenin is an anagram?" he asks his visitor.

She just smiles and says nothing.

2. The Sale

Out in the open-air market there is a big sign that says SEMI-ANIMAL SALE. It is for the tourists from New Zealand and Australia.

"Look, isn't that cute?" says a banker from Auckland. "They've made a mistake on the sign."

But as the group of tourists gets closer, they see it is no mistake. On sale in the market are centaurs, sphinxes and satyrs.

All of the tourists crowd around, astounded at the semi-animals.

An elderly lady from Sydney says, "But I thought these were just mythical creatures!"

The Cambodian merchants smile. Only one of them talks English well. He says to the crowd, "At our rural cooperative we have gorgons if you like."

"Gorgons?" says a red-faced Australian. "What do you feed them, gorgonzola cheese?"

Fool, thinks the Cambodian merchant who can speak English. I know one semi-animal I would love to sell you. You would love owning a griffin, an insipid creature with the head of an eagle, the body of a lion and the mind of a talk-show host.

None of the tourists buys any of the semi-animals. A young teacher from Melbourne would like to purchase a satyr, but her fiance will not let her. "They are not as smart as the average bear," he tells her.

3. The Scholar

"And here," says the Minister of Culture to the visitor, leading her by the arm, "here is our finest scholar, Duk Sup."

The visitor shakes the hand of the young scholar, who cannot be more than seventeen. He has just the beginnings of an adolescent mustache. He smiles wildly.

"Wine opera wishes sure as soda," Duk Sup recites.

The visitor is confused, looks at the Minister of Culture.

"A great English poet," says the Minister. "He has learned it by heart."

Duk Sup nods enthusiastically.

"Western education has a few things to teach us," the Minister tells the visitor. "But only a few."

"I especially like your films of the forties and the thirties," says Duk Sup.

The visitor nods. She is only a journalist, but she is supposedly representing her culture. There is more uncomfortable Cambodian silence.

"I have sent away for membership in American film society," Duk Sup tells the woman. "Phi Beta Capra, I believe it is called . . . . I wish to join very much."

The Minister of Culture clears his throat haughtily. "Is not for spying purposes," he tries to reassure the visitor. "Is true love for cinema."

Duk Sup's eyes light up. "Yes. Especially James Stewart."

The visitor finds herself puzzled again. She turns to the Minister of Culture. "You approve of James Stewart?"

"Oh yes. Certainly. He is an excellent actor and we find his mannerisms very endearing."

The visitor smiles and nods.

4. The Collective

Another sign in Cambodian as the tourists make their way to the rural collective. But next to the native sign is a translation in English.

NO TRESPASSING, says the sign. ALL TRESPASSERS WILL BE SUBJECT TO THE PREDICATE "ARE TRESPASSSING."

"Charming," says the elderly lady from Sydney.

The residents of the collective rise up and greet the tourists. They throw rice at them.

"Western custom," says the guide to the Australians and the New Zealanders. "They wish to let you know they appreciate you as much as a newly married couple."

"Just charming," says the elderly lady.

5. *The Misfits*

The visitor is taking notes. She is writing in her notebook. She is being lectured to by Pol Pot.

"The misfits, you see," Pol Pot tells her. "They must be contradictions."

The visitor doesn't understand.

"We don't want people to be contradictions here," says the leader of revolutionary Kampuchea. "We must separate them from our society."

"And how do you do that?" asks the visitor, her pen poised on her paper.

"By contradicting their contradictions," says Pol Pot.

What does that mean? the visitor thinks but does not say aloud.

Pol Pot coughs, spits some phlegm into a white handkerchief. "Like that," he tells the visitor. He means like the phlegm.

6. *The Ex-Prostitutes*

The ex-prostitutes live in a recycling center. Here they learn to sew. Gradually they give up their Western ways: their decadent clothing and their makeup. No makeup is allowed in the new people's republic, not even khmer rouge, which used to be permitted.

7. *Angkor Wat*

"Can we see Angkor Wat?" asks the elderly woman from Sydney. "I'm sure it must be charming."

She is sharing her bed with the tourist guide.

"What anger?"

"The temple," she insists. "The ancient temple."

The guide smiles at her, rolls over to her side of the bed, touches her on the forehead. "*This* ancient temple," he laughs. And laughs and laughs.

The lady does *not* say, "Charming."

8. The Meeting of the Minds

On a dusky road which used to be filled with fighting Viet Cong and American soldiers in the years 1970 and 1971, the tourists' bus breaks down. They manage to flag down a car in two days. In the car are Pol Pot and his female visitor. Pol Pot gets out and tells the tourists that help is on the way. They cheer him with good Australian and New Zealander words.

Pol Pot gets back into the car. He loves to handle a stick shift.

"Where are you going to stop for help for those people?" the visitor asks the leader of the revolutionary regime.

He laughs.

9. The Annihilation of Lust

"Lust is completely eliminated in Kampuchea," says Pol Pot. "Our people have realized it is nothing. You Westerners, this is all you think of and you live your life in constant pursuit of. And then in the end, nothing is left."

"Nothing?" says the visitor. She is more comfortable with him now, since their night in the countryside together. "It *is* everything. Almost."

Pol Pot laughs, pats the visitor on her thigh. He looks at her with non-lust. He nods. He whispers: "All this and herpes 2?"

Suddenly the visitor finds herself feeling very frightened.

10. The Refugees

"We've got to find a nook or a cranny to hide out in tonight or we're doomed," says one refugee to his wife.

"But I don't see a cranny," she cries. "And I certainly don't Sihanouk."

11. The Return

The visitor is no longer a visitor. She is back in her own country, trying to catch up on the headlines of the newspaper for which she works:

MAY BEEF PRICES RISE

BEGIN TALKS SET

ELECTION RETURNS FROM TURKEY TRIP

Her roommate asks her what she knows about the missing tourists from New Zealand and Australia.

"Not much," says the ex-visitor.

"This trip," says her roommate. "It affected you a lot, didn't it?"

"Not much," says the ex-visitor.

"Are you sorry you went?"

"Not much."

"Are you glad you're back home?"

"Not much."

The roommate sighs. "What was Pol Pot like?"

"Not much," replies the ex-visitor.

The roommate knows that it is her own turn to be frightened now. "Tell me, Joanne," she asks, "what *really* happened in Cambodia?"

And of course the answer: "Not much."

12. The Deaths

"All of them are dead, Comrade," reports the Minister of Culture to his leader.

"Very good," says Pol Pot. "How many is that now—including the semi-animals?"

"*All* of them. Everyone except you and I."

"Even Duk Sup and the sign-makers?"

"Especially the sign-makers. You know, Comrade, we found this sign on the edge of a settlement near Tien Tien: WE LIKE GRILS . . ."

"Yes? So?" Pol Pot is impatient.

"Underneath it was another sign: BUT WHAT ABOUT US GIRLS?"

Pol Pot laughs heartily.

"Go Not to Lethe" Celebrates Its 27th Anniversary

"GO NOT TO LETHE" is having a birthday. The long-running IBS daytime serial will mark its 27th year on June 4, 1978, and *Soap Opera Journal* has gone behind the scenes of one of your favorite shows to tell you the story of its past and what you can expect to look forward to in the future.

"Go Not to Lethe's" Richard Grayson has always been daytime TV's answer to radio's "Romance of Helen Trent," "Stella Dallas," and other heroine-oriented shows. TV watchers have been engrossed for more than a score of years by Richard's unshakable faith that he'll find true happiness, despite his many troubles and those of the people around him.

Few daytime serials can boast of having only one star, but "Go Not to Lethe" can: Grayson Richards. He's on the program an average of four times a week. Viewers have watched him live through grammar school, high school and college, the deaths of relatives, the loss of lovers, the threats to his parents' happiness, and the troubles of his many friends. Twenty-seven years is a long time, and Grayson Richards and his audience are all practically family by now.

Sitting in his kitchen, where his mother is serving tea, Grayson jokes about his special daytime-TV status: "I've told others this before, but I'm probably the world's oldest living male ingenue." Oldest? Perhaps—but somehow still youthful as the ever-boyish Richard, Grayson has a firm physique, wears clothes (off and on the show) with a casual grace, has tanned but acne-sprinkled skin, and pure, deep hazel eyes. Those eyes, the haunting shape of his mouth, and the slightly recessed chin are the most instantly recognizable things about Grayson. Back in 1951, when this young man was only a newborn infant, he and "Go Not to Lethe" met daytime television audiences for the first time, and—seasoned and made somewhat more interesting by age and the complexities of a well-developed personality—they are still on the air today.

"Many viewers think that Richie Grayson and I are one and the same person and believe that I just make up his words on the show myself. I think that's the greatest compliment an actor can receive, to be told that he is so convincing that he *must* be living out his own life on television. Actually, Richard, as a character, is very dear to me because I've lived with him for so long and because we are so much alike. We both want to do what is right, and we've both been growing more mature as the years have flown by—perhaps we're different only in that Richard is so much more concerned with the people around him than I can allow myself to be. I'm more of a loner than Richie. I prefer to spend my time sitting quietly at home writing. I have little social life outside of my friendships with the actors on 'Lethe.' I suppose I would like to have other friends, but I have a greater need to spend my time alone being creative."

As he spoke, Grayson's mother, Mrs. Richards, came into the room to tell Grayson that his ex-girlfriend was on the phone. After he spoke to her and returned to the kitchen, Grayson announced, "Well you know, I'm still good friends with *all* of my old lovers!" Let's see—he was referring to Sylvia Carroll, who played Carol Silberman, Richie's first girlfriend; and to Robin Strassman, who caused a lot of trouble for Richie in her time; and to Hope Rosenthal, Richie's longest-running partner; and finally to Richard's current lover and his first homosexual one, Tom Bevins. "I adore Tom," says Grayson. "I hope we can stay together a long time. And I loved Hope Rosenthal; I was sorry when she decided to leave the show. But I'm friends with them all."

Richard and Grayson's lives have intermeshed, obviously—but then, real life and soap opera fiction tend to do that. "Well, it's been a steady job and it's helped make me a nice home for myself," says Grayson, underplaying as always, whenever he is asked to sum up his long career on "Go Not to Lethe." Obviously, Grayson has taken "Lethe" and Richard as more than just an acting job. For Grayson, Richard is a real person who must be reckoned with by other real people. For example, the writers occasionally forget who Richard really is and make him too pushy or a shade too possessive, and it is always Grayson who cares enough about the show and his viewers to stick up for Richie's true personality. He knows exactly how it has changed through the years and how it hasn't. It is a remarkable feat of self-control on Grayson Richards' part, for in recent years he and Richard Grayson have parted company on several distinct points of personality makeup.

Grayson and Richard both were the oldest of three sons, both lived in Brooklyn, and both were heroes in the way they conducted their affairs with other people. Both spent a great deal of time in psychotherapy and both spent almost as much time worrying about the troubles and welfare of those around them. But at the studio, Grayson sometimes retreats into his own little world, while some people around him wonder if they aren't being snubbed by Grayson and Richard. "These days," says Linda Connors, who has played the part of Richie's best friend for nearly twenty years, "some people think Grayson's aloof because he may not join the other actors when they are socializing but goes off into a corner and just thinks." Grayson himself admits that occasionally he tends to use playing the part of Richard as a way of escaping—and, as Jack Shapiro (who plays Richard's grandfather) says, "Grayson *never* stops working . . . his attitude has made him the most thoroughly professional person I've ever worked with."

On June 4, 1951, viewers first saw Richard Grayson and "Go Not to Lethe"—the show's title comes from the opening line of John Keats's "Ode to Melancholy"—in a fifteen-minute black-and-white live broadcast. The story at first was simple. Richard was the newly-born son of Marilyn and Daniel Grayson, a young Jewish couple living in Brooklyn, a large borough of New York City. Richard's parents were happily married, though somewhat hovered over by their own parents, who lived not far away. After three years, another son was born to the Graysons—Marc—and about seven years after the show started, Linda Connors came into the story as Richard's classmate. Throughout the years, hundreds of actors have come and gone on "Lethe," but no one outside the Grayson family has achieved the popularity of Linda Connors. When a new actress playing the part appeared in 1971, the audiences wouldn't stand for it, and the old Linda had to be brought back—much to the relief of the viewing public. Linda has supplied much of the light comedy on the show; she is always around with a smile, a joke, and an outstretched hand when things get a bit rough for Richard and his family. This comedy touch distinguished "Go Not to Lethe" from the scores of unrelieved melodramatic serials which preceded it. Currently, Linda Connors is amusing audiences as an editor at the magazine *Seventeen,* still trying to work out her wacky off-again, on-again romance with sculptor David Detweiler (played by Detlev Davids).

"Go Not to Lethe" expanded to half an hour in 1956, went to color ten years later, and became the first hour-long serial drama in 1970. Anthropologist Margaret Mead, herself a GNTL fan, ascribed the show's popularity to the fact that it's "closer to reality than either movies or nighttime TV because on 'Lethe' even the heroes like Richie and his father can have weaknesses, suffer breakdowns, and die." Also, Mead said, the show offers not escape but identification: "People can pick out certain characters in the story—Marilyn, Daniel, Richard, Linda Connors, Grandpa Jack—who remind them of their own mothers, fathers, sons, daughters, grandparents." A viewer once angrily said to Grayson Richards: "I want to slap Robin Strassman's face for being so mean to you because you remind me of my own brother."

This identification often extends to the actors on the show as well. Veteran actress Beadie Shapiro tells an incredible but true story: "I had been playing Richie's Grandma Beadie for five years. One afternoon I returned home from the studio and began poking around in my clothes closet. Suddenly I reeled from the shock. Every article of clothing in that closet was Grandma Beadie's, not mine. Every dress and coat was exactly like her—dowdy and ultraconservative. I panicked and scooped up all the clothes in my arms and threw them out! I had forgotten who I was. I had become Grandma Beadie!"

Jack Shapiro, who plays Grandma Beadie's folksy husband Grandpa Jack, tells of the time he had gotten off from "Lethe" to appear in an off-Broadway play. As soon as he made his entrance on stage, a woman in the audience stood up and shouted for all the world to hear, "Why, I know you, Grandpa Jack! . . . What on earth are you doing up there?" Jack swears that another time, on his way to the studio one Monday morning, he was followed and stopped on the Brooklyn Bridge by a policeman who wanted to know what was going to happen next to Richie.

In the course of over a quarter of a century, Richard and his family have found themselves well off, on the brink of poverty, the managers of a hotel in the Borscht Belt, owners of a pants manufacturing concern, involved in a low exacta riot at Yonkers Raceway and the management of an unsuccessful flea market. Currently Richard's father, Daniel, is just getting on his feet again after a year of unemployment which led to much frustration on his part and a brief separation from wife Marilyn, who didn't know how to assuage her husband's anguish. Richard, having gone through years of public school, college and graduate school, is now eking out a meager living as a part-time college English instructor; of course his big dream is to become an experimental fiction writer, but there are many roadblocks in his way.

The first real tragedy on the series occurred when real life and soap opera life cruelly merged. On June 17, 1956, Yetta Saretsky died suddenly and the producers of "Go Not to Lethe" were thrown into a panic. How could they replace Yetta, who had played Richie's beloved great-grandmother, Bubbe Ita? They tried out a few elderly actresses, but no one was right for the part. So a month after Yetta Saretsky's death, the writers had Bubbe Ita die on the show. Ironically, it was as if all the events surrounding Yetta's death were being repeated in fiction. The reaction of the characters—Grandpa Jack saying, "I can still hardly believe it!"; people calling one another and exchanging stories about Bubbe Ita and how wonderful she was and what an inspiration to the family; Richie's own childish confusion at the death—was precisely what happened off camera when the news of Yetta's death hit Grayson and the other characters.

Several years ago "Go Not to Lethe" viewers suffered for months while Uncle Harry (played by Hal Harris) was dying of lung cancer. Still, the fans had hope: they wrote hundreds of letters of great concern to "Lethe's" producers and writers to spare him. Uncle Harry—a bit of a con man when he was first introduced on the show in 1966 as Aunt Rose's second husband—died anyway, just a week before his daughter's wedding. Hundreds more letters poured in, angry letters this time: "How could you let Uncle Harry die? I've liked your show until now . . ." It was as if people were saying, "I've liked *life*—until now." But in the end no viewer really blamed "Go Not to Lethe." "It was just *life,*" as Grayson Richards has said.

The show's ratings were at their peak in the years 1968–1969, while Richard had his nervous breakdown following high-school graduation. For a year he barely left his room. Grayson Richards's portrayal of seventeen-year-old Richard, cracking up in the face of agoraphobia, sexual confusion and compulsive anxiety, was nothing short of remarkable. Viewers tuned in week after week to see one "mad" scene after another, brilliantly underplayed by Grayson. Unfortunately, one result of all this fine acting was that Grayson began to develop some of Richie's symptoms; he would become nauseated in public places and feared that he would die if he traveled too far from home. Luckily, at about the time Grayson's problems were mimicking those of his character, the writers began to tire of the nervous breakdown theme and had Richard gradually recover and start college. "If it had gone on another two months," says Grayson, "I might have ended up in worse shape than Richard."

The low point of the show came when ratings plummeted in 1974 following the voluntary departure of two of the audience's favorite actresses, those playing Richie's popular girlfriend Hope Rosenthal and his witty, gentle psychotherapist, Mrs. Ehrlichman. The writers of "Lethe" did not want to bring on a new therapist (Richie had been in therapy for eight years with several different psychologists) nor a new girlfriend either—right away. (In October of 1974, Hope Rosenthal had a press conference in which she said she would not return to the part of Richie's girlfriend "unless my father were in a Nazi concentration camp and only my reappearance as Hope would get him out.") With Richie's life and that of his family in low key, the show's writers faced a dilemma: how to build up interest in the show. Then a brainstorm hit. June Grant had been introduced three years earlier as the girlfriend of Richie's friend Keith Milstein; her father opposed the romance, reviling Keith as "that hippie Jew." She was only supposed to be on the show for six weeks, but audience reaction was so favorable to the willowy blonde actress that she was kept on indefinitely as a minor character. Why not, the writers decided, bring June Grant's family onto GNTL? According to the story line, June's bigoted father had run out on the family following his retirement from the Transit Authority, leaving June, her mother, and brother somewhat happier but concerned about their futures. The viewers immediately fell in love with the Grant family and their special brand of zaniness, and new plots were devised around them. Brother Jack Grant skinned cats alive, had trouble graduating high school, and was always getting himself into hot water with his teenage girlfriend Angela. June Grant herself left Keith for awhile, but following his brother's suicide and through Richie's loving intervention, they were reunited, although the future looks rocky for them. Perhaps the most beloved Grant is the delightful and homespun Mrs. Grant, whose unpretentious and complaisant personality and sloppy housekeeping (she flicks ashes on her own living room floor) make her a wonderful contrast to Richard's mother Marilyn, who is forever telling her family to put away dishes or dust the shelves. And for three years, the show's Christmas episode has taken place over dinner at the Grants'—it looks like this will be a "Lethe" tradition for years to come.

"Go Not to Lethe's" only black star, Joan Claire, plays Claire Jones, Marilyn Grayson's cleaning woman for the past decade. In the space of ten years, Claire has been fired and rehired twice, seen two husbands die, been robbed many times, gone through a hysterectomy, been stuck on many subway trains, and participated in more than a score of hilarious scenes with Richard's ultra-tidy mother. There was a funny incident when Joan Claire came home after taping a particular episode and found her *own* cleaning woman walking out on her. "I can't work for a woman like you! To treat Mrs. Grayson the way you do! You ought to be ashamed of yourself!" It was no use explaining. The housekeeper had been watching the show and refused to believe that Joan wasn't Claire. Fiction won out.

Real people *do* sometimes appear on the show—even famous real people. When the storyline called for Richie's college friend Mark Vishinsky to be elected a delegate to the Democratic National Convention in 1972, and for Richie and Mark to go to Miami Beach to take part in the proceedings (the shows were shot on location in Florida), such prominent politicians as John Lindsay, Hubert Humphrey and even Presidential nominee George McGovern agreed to be on hand to play themselves. These shows were very popular indeed with GNTL lovers.

It was *not* very pleasant for Sylvia Carroll at one time. She played the now much-loved, though once-hated, Carol Silberman, and she was often accosted by angry women who slapped her and called her a slut. She had to have police protection going to and from the studio when the character she portrayed was leaving Richie to marry his good friend, Paul Schwartz. Now, of course, Carol is divorced from her homosexual husband and living in Madison, Wisconsin. When Carol was gang-raped on the show recently, the actress received many expressions of concern from well-wishers—a tribute to her fine acting job of making Carol not just a shallow villainess but a maturing, love-starved, overweight woman. (Incidentally, "Go Not to Lethe" portrayed the rape and its aftermath realistically, with Carol's friends and her ex-husband convincing her to just forget the incident and not face the humiliation of a court case.)

Perhaps not so surprisingly, there *have* been occasions when viewers, by their pleading letters, did what they could not do for Uncle Harry and saved the life of a character in the show. When Tillie Greenwald, one of the original "Lethe" cast members, appeared as Richard's bitter, interfering Grandma Tillie, she was only supposed to cause a lot of trouble for a while and then die of cancer of the colon. When it came time for her demise, viewers simply wouldn't have it. After being swamped with letters and telegrams to "save Grandma Tillie's life," the producers did just that, and the actress is still on the show today, making occasional appearances as a now-senile nursing-home resident, a burden to the entire Grayson family.

Of course, everyone agrees that in the end the show rests on one man: Grayson Richards. Grayson says he doesn't have the kind of power on "Lethe" that other people assume he has. "I have no idea of what is going to happen in the story. I can influence the producers sometimes, but only when I feel very strongly about something, and that doesn't happen often. I remember I didn't want to have Richard get a job after he graduated college, so I suggested that Richie switch from being a Poli Sci major and go to graduate school in English. It was one of the few times I influenced a story line."

Through the years, Grayson has learned so much about the finer points of putting together a soap opera that he's always being called on to help out when serious technical and creative problems arise. Once a director, in the middle of a taping, discovered he was five minutes short and became frantic. How could he invent five minutes of material that wasn't in the script? He asked Grayson to help out, and in shorthand he wrote a five-minute scene between Ivy Siegel and himself. In the conversation Ivy told Richie that she was saddened by Carol Silberman's marriage and expressed the hope that she herself would never fall into the trap of conventional marriage. It turned out to be one of the best scenes of the day.

Where, fans might ask, is "Go Not to Lethe" going? First the good news: wherever it is going, it is going strong. GNTL is now the second-highest-rated daytime TV show and it shows all signs of running at least another twenty-seven years. Fans of "Lethe" can look forward to new adventures as Richie matures and explores new aspects of himself and of life; his relationship with the boyish Tom Bevins is only one case in point. What will happen to all of our favorite characters: Richie, his parents, his grandparents, Linda Connors, the Grants, Claire, Mark Vishinsky, Carol Silberman? The writers of the show won't tell us, despite *Soap Opera Journal*'s insistent and penetrating queries. Grayson Richards provides us with what is perhaps the definitive answer to those who ponder the futures of all of those on the show: "Just keep watching, and you'll find out the future—the same as we who appear on the show."

The First Annual James V. Forrestal Memorial Lecture

My roommate Angela Cozzarelli is practicing to be *the* great intellectual figure of the 1990s. I have loved Angela ever since I met her at a Newman Club picnic back in the days when Dinah Shore ruled the earth. That day she told me under a willow tree that she would never marry because of her ambition. I confessed to her that I would never marry because I liked boys. (What else would a nice Jewish boy be doing at a Newman Club picnic? I was watching my heartthrob Eddie Dugan play softball without a shirt.)

Now we are older and we live together. We have separate rooms. Angela's room is filled with her books and my room is filled with Angela's books. If you are preparing to be a great intellectual figure, books come in handy. I don't read very much myself.

If I could properly describe Angela to you, you wouldn't forget her all the days of your life. She wears glasses too big for her face and always looks as though her hair has just been washed and towel-dried. I am the one with the blow-dryer in this non-nuclear (or unclear) family.

When I got out of college, I got into a graduate program in sociology. I did research. I took classes. I had a teaching assistantship, passed my orals, wrote my dissertation. Finally I got my doctorate, the Ph.D. that follows my name and a comma. I sent out 427 resumes to various departments of sociology in the United States and Canada. There was just one reply. I went for an interview.

"What did you do your dissertation on?" the fat florid chairwoman asked me. " 'The Adaptive Patterns of Concentration Camp Survivors in a Rural American Setting,' " I told her. "The last thing this department needs," she sniffed, "is another Holocaust-accountant."

So I rewrote my resume. I look very young so I took eight years off my life and wrote that I had just gotten out of high school. Luckily I look vaguely jockish shrugged into my jeans and my nylon taffeta warmup jacket. And I got my job at Middlebrook Mall. ("Middle*brow* Mall," Angela calls it.)

I am with the security force. Mostly I just walk around the mall. "Handsome fellow like you," said my boss, Mr. Bixby. "Give the people something to look at. Wear French jeans and nice tops. Get your hair cut like John Travolta in that movie. You'll do fine."

And so I have; me, Adlai Stevenson Rosenthal, cute kid with a doctorate. I look like one of those eighteen-year-olds who play the son in a family sit-com, the kind of young actors who end up on the covers of *16* and *Tiger Beat.* Every shopping center needs people to walk around and be stared at; that is part of the reason people come.

Other things I do:

I attempt to find lost babies. Best place to look: near the red-and-yellow DNA chain sculpture. The babies are attracted to the double helix. Angela wants to do a study of it someday.

I go for gasoline when someone in the parking lot has run out.

I look out for a gang of teenage girls in identical Farrah hairstyles who rob old people.

I make sure there are no hand-lettered signs anywhere. Mr. Bixby says they are bad for morale.

Angela, what does she do? She stayed in the academic racket. She teaches remedial English to Third Worlders who have the edge in Affirmative Action. Angela has one disciple already, a former student, Placenta Smith.

"Marriage is too important to base it on love," says Angela, and Placenta nods in agreement.

"The ancient Greeks wrote in boustrophedon, 'as the ox plows,' " Angela lectures, and Placenta takes copious notes.

"*Fame* comes from a Middle English word meaning to *talk,*" Angela tells Placenta. "Therefore, quiet people rarely become famous."

Angela and Placenta both hope to be famous one day. As for me, well, I just want to be around to see it happen.

We are sitting around the apartment one Saturday evening, Angela, Placenta, and I.

"What shall we do?" says Angela, closing her book.

Placenta and I think, or pretend to.

"We could go to CBGB's," I suggest. "They've got a small band of Zionist hoodlums playing there tonight."

"Not tonight," says Angela. "I'm not in the mood for punk."

"We could study up on epistemology," Placenta offers.

Angela and I look at her.

"Well, it was just a thought," she says defensively. And then: "Why are there Saturday nights altogether? Do you think there will be Saturday nights in heaven?"

I take a sip of Pepsi Light. "Certainly not," I tell her.

Angela is thinking. "What if there were no weekends?" she asks. "We could just have five days in a week. After Friday, Monday could come. We'd have . . . seventy-three weeks a year. Each date would fall out on the same day every year."

"What about leap years?" I ask her.

"Um, a special holiday every four years. Separate from the rest of the week."

Placenta shifts in her seat. "But people want leisure," she says.

Angela and I look at her again. Placenta gives up the thought.

"No more Saturday or Sunday," Placenta thinks aloud. "It might work."

"It just might."

I cough, a small one, nothing to worry about. "Why are there seven days in a week anyway? There's no actual reason for it, is there?"

"God," Angela says.

"Oh, *Him,*" I say.

"He should have stopped after fish and fowl on the fifth day," Angela tells us. "Then He wouldn't have had to take a whole day out to rest."

So we do nothing on Saturday night.

The next day, I find that Angela has her nose in a book.

"If mules can't reproduce," she asks me, "do you think they can be cloned?"

"Mules can't reproduce?"

"Of course not, silly," Angela smiles. "They're products of two different species and therefore always sterile."

"Oh," I say, getting some Kraft American Cheese Singles out of the refrigerator, "I didn't know."

She goes back to her book. "Your mother called while you were out," she tells me.

"Not my mother," I say.

"Yes, your mother."

"*Moth-er,*" I repeat aloud, then stuff a slice of cheese in my mouth. "An ugly word, no?"

"Most languages have words for *mother* that are imitative of sucking noises at the breast," Angela drawls, without looking up.

"*Mm-mm,*" I say, getting out a gherkin pickle. "I should have thought of that myself. Why *not* the breast?" I sit down at the bridge table in the kitchen and begin to make a sandwich.

An hour later Angela comes into the room. "Are you still eating?" she asks me.

I notice the book at her side, and I say, "Are you still reading?"

"Come here," she whispers. She motions to the bathroom, and of course I follow. Placenta is already in there. Angela locks the door behind us. We are silent for a moment. Angela sits on the toilet seat, Placenta and I on the edge of the tub.

Finally Angela says softly, "I think it's fear of success."

I nod. "That must be it."

Placenta, confused, wants to know what's going on.

"Isn't it obvious?" says Angela. "Where's your motivation?"

Placenta shrugs. "I guess I don't have any."

"Sh," I say. "Do you want *him* to hear us?"

"*He's* in bad shape," Angela says. "We have to do something."

"Look, *he'll* figure out what do with us," I tell her.

"Not this time," Angela says. "Besides, I can't wait for *him* to think up a plot. If I have to read that damn genetics book one more time, I'll throw up."

"At least that would be some action," Placenta says.

Angela and I have to give her one of those looks again. And then she says, "See, that's the third time in just a few pages that we've had to give you that look. Something's terribly wrong."

Placenta starts to cry. "I'm getting scared."

"Hush," I say. "Do you want *him* to hear us?"

"See, Adlai," says Angela, "You just said that a few lines back. The situation is getting desperate."

"Oh Lord, oh Lord," cries Placenta. Then she looks at me: "You're the narrator, *you* do something."

I shrug. I know it's a cliché, but what else can I do? I am scared but trying not to show it. "How could this have happened?" I think aloud. "This started out so promisingly. I thought the first page was so good."

"It was, it was," Angela assures me. "*He* set up a pretty funny situation. Anyway, it had possibilities . . . ."

"I liked the line 'shrugged into my jeans,' " says Placenta. Already she is looking less and less like a black woman.

"All right," I sigh, trying to be the man of the bathroom. I don't say that line because I'm sure it would be followed by an even worse one. Secretly I am not so sure *he's* not watching us. Don't panic, I tell myself. This too shall pass.

"Think of some ideas," says Angela. "Quick, before *he* catches on that something's up."

"The mall could be blown up by terrorists," I say. "And me with it. All those Stay-Free Maxi-Pads and down jackets and digital clock radios and smoke detectors and electric woks."

"Right on!" shouts Placenta, then realizes she is too loud. In a whisper she says, "A stunning indictment of American materialism."

"Trite," says Angela. We always listen to Angela.

Time is running out.

Despite myself, I *am* beginning to panic. I have to admit to myself that I never believed in that scene at the mall at all. I begin to pull at my short hair.

"Keep calm, keep calm," says Angela. "How about I become a famous intellectual figure and you assassinate me?"

"No motivation," I say, my voice cracking.

"Woe is me, woe is me," moans Placenta. She falls backwards into the bathtub. A sure sign that the author is losing his grip.

"Okay," Angela sighs. "Forget about her, she was only in the story to provide someone for us to talk to. It's you and me, Adlai, we've got to come up with something fast."

"Sex!" I shout. "When in doubt, sex!"

"No," she says.

"*He* only said I liked boys," I tell her. "Liking boys doesn't mean impotent with women."

"I'm not in the mood right now, if you don't mind—not with this sword of Damocles over our heads. If you want to bring back Eddie What's-his-name from the Newman Club picnic, that's all right with me, but I don't think we have time to establish him as a viable character . . . ."

"Hell, we ain't even viable ourselves!" cries Placenta.

"Shut her up," I say. "I thought her name was a kind of racist joke anyway."

"And *your* name?" Angela shouts at me. Her face is ugly now. "Adlai Stevenson Rosenthal—come off it! *I'm* the only one with a decent name in this story. *And* the only one with a brain!"

"I've got more brains in my little pinky than you have in your whole body," I tell her. And then suddenly I look down and I *do*—there is a silicone chip in my hand.

Placenta notices it, too. She grabs her heart. "Saved by modern technology!" she sings.

"Not so fast," says Angela, who then realizes her saying "Not so fast" is a sign of what dire straits we are in. I try to unlock the bathroom door but it doesn't work.

"We've got only one chance in a million," I say desperately.

"It just might work," Placenta says haltingly.

"All right, give it a try," says Angela querulously. "All these adverbs are driving me out of my mind."

"Okay," I say, taking a deep breath to ward off any nearby adverbs. "We've got to feed all the data in this story so far into . . ."

"MY GOD!" screamed Placenta, a blood-curdling sound. "Your silicone chip's GONE!"

Sure enough, my hands were empty except for a slice of American cheese.

"Not only that," said Angela, "but we've slipped into the past tense."

"Is this the end of Placenta Smith?" Placenta asked with emotion or without emotion; it was getting hard to tell one from the other.

"There are only a few minutes left in this story," I said. "Quick, think up something to save us! A line of dialogue, a description, a piece of narrative, *anything* . . ."

"Um," said Angela, "a pun: We're passing Carl Jung's grave and you say, 'He may only be dust and bones now, but he was Jung once.' "

"An interesting word," Placenta cried out. "*Agamist:* a person who is against marriage."

"Another pun," shot back Angela. "We get killed in an earthquake through no fault of our own."

"Why the hell are all your puns about death?"

"I guess it's because I feel it coming on. We're on the way out."

"I feel it too."

"Look, there aren't any 'he saids' anymore. You can't tell whose line of dialogue it is . . ."

"What about the title of the story?"

" 'The First Annual James V. Forrestal Memorial Lecture'? What about it?"

"It's got to be worked into the story before it ends."

"Oh, God! Who can think about that?"

"Look, we've got to. If we're going to go, we at least want to clear up *that.* This is Angela Cozzarelli speaking. I am about to give the first annual James V. Forrestal Memorial Lecture. Here goes: Forrestal was Secretary of Defense under Truman and he went crazy in his last year in office. He was depressed, manic, paranoid . . . He thought Israeli agents were following him around everywhere . . ."

"They were!"

"Shut up, you faggot kike! —And when he was forced to resign he cracked up and tried to commit suicide in florida they sent him to bethesda naval hospital to recover—

weve lost all punctuation except exclamation marks!

shut up i said james v forrestal was in an unguarded room on the sixteenth floor of the hospital when he was copying out lines from sophocles ajax

what lines

worn by the waste of time comfortless nameless hopeless save

save us

save in the dark prospect of the yawning grave

oh god im sorry for everything

A NOTE ON THE TYPE

Books on violence in America are usually set on the Linotype in Janson, a recutting made direct from type cast from matrices long thought to have been made by the Dutchman Anton Janson, who was a practicing type founder in Leipzig during the years 1668–87. However, it has now been conclusively demonstrated that these types are actually the work of Nicholas Kis (1650–1702), a Hungarian who probably learned his trade from the master Dutch type founder Kirk Voskens. Janson (which is a misnomer and should rightfully be called Kis) is an excellent example of the influential and sturdy Dutch types that prevailed in England up to the time of William Caslon. John Updike, an American author of Dutch descent, insists that all his novels be set in Janson.

John Cheever's novels are set in Monticello, although he too prefers Janson. But Cheever is a reticent man, and does not like to make an issue of it. Besides, Monticello is a Linotype revival of the original Binny & Ronaldson Roman No. 1, and as such, it is heir to a long tradition of excellence. So Cheever has nothing to be ashamed of when critics read his prose in Monticello, a transitional type design embodying features of both Bulmer and Baskerville.

Few people have noticed the similarities between the fiction of James M. Cain and the poetry of Wallace Stevens. Of course, the common denominator is that both are set in Electra, a typeface designed by W(illiam) A(ddison) Dwiggins (1880–1956) for the Mergenthaler Company. At one time Dwiggins shared an office with Rudolph Ruzicka, but it is difficult to gauge just who influenced whom, if anyone.

Exquisite pornography is often set in Granjon, a type named in compliment to Robert Granjon, but neither a copy of a classic face or an entirely original creation. Actually Granjon more closely resembles the types used by the somewhat disreputable Claude Garamond (1510–61) than it does any type of Granjon, who began his career as a typecutter in 1523, following an unsuccessful stint as a poultry farmer. The boldest and most original designer of his time, Granjon was often pounced upon by jealous rivals.

This book is set in Baskerville.